A Killer of a Cruise

A Julia Greene Travel Mystery

by

Linda Clayton

For information, email Cozy Cat Press, cozycatpress@aol.com or visit our website at: www.cozycatpress.com

COZY CAT
P R E S S

ISBN: 978-1-946063-64-9
Printed in the United States of America

10 9 8 7 6 5 4 3 2 1

For Carolyn, Tim, Sophie and Beckett, who were there.

CHAPTER ONE

I need a map to find my way around the Golden Eagle. The 110,000-ton cruise ship is a huge floating hotel with fancy shops, restaurants, a spa, swimming pools, and two thousand passengers—all spread over nineteen decks. It is awesomely overwhelming, and I am loving every second of my stay onboard. So is Olivia Duncan, my best friend and business partner.

She and I own Little Bites, a lunchroom and pastry shop in Wake Forest, North Carolina. It took us a long time to save up enough money for this trip. For instance, a portion of quiche costs $2.95 at our establishment, even if you order extras like bacon, brie, and kale. Out of that we have to pay for the eggs and veggies, plus compensate our wait staff, which at the moment consists of Olivia, Molly—a young mother who helps us part time—and me. So Olivia and I are determined to enjoy every second of this long-anticipated trip to Alaska.

For eight sweet days, we will have no mixers exploding and sending cupcake batter to the cciling, no cranky oven that only heats properly if I get down on my knees and beg, and no bills, customers, phone calls, or anything else that makes us want to go up on the roof and jump off. Don't get me wrong. We love our little lunchroom, but a relaxing break is good for the soul. And a little pampering never hurt anyone. A friendly steward cleans our room, and terrific chefs prepare awesome meals. In other words, we're livin' large.

We have a veranda stateroom on Deck 11, which is an amazing luxury for us, and reservations tonight at the Trattoria Italiana, a restaurant on the ship. In the evenings before dinner, Olivia and I sit out on the veranda with our feet propped on the railing, Bloody Marys in our hands, and marvel at how lucky we are. We're only on the second day of our Alaskan cruise, but I'm already wishing the trip could last forever. Olivia, however, is more fashion-conscious and won't be upset when the cruise ends. The sea air frizzes her hair.

Now that I think about it, it's a miracle that I, Julia Greene, am here at all and not buried in musty archives in a remote Egyptian town. My life certainly veered off the course I'd charted.

Several years ago, I graduated from Columbia with a degree in art history and a minor in Egyptian art—the latter sending my poor mother into an absolute frenzy of anxiety. At graduation we stood on the dusty New York sidewalk as a gentle breeze swirled gum wrappers and other debris around our ankles, and I listened to her worry for the ten thousandth time. "But what will you actually do, dear? Don't you have to go to Egypt to work in your field?"

No, because I had already accepted a teaching position at a private school in Boston, but I hadn't told Mother yet. I intended to tell her after lunch. Mark, the man of my dreams and hopefully my soon-to-be husband, was joining us. I had my life figured out: a white colonial, two dogs, Mark's job as a lawyer—maybe even a baby.

At Tavern on the Green, I ordered wonderful mussels in some kind of garlic wine sauce with a mystical salad of exotic greens, sliced almonds, and feta cheese. Mark ordered a hamburger, which should have tipped me off because he loved good food, but I was euphoric and just a bit tipsy from the very decent sauvignon blanc he ordered. Mother was so relieved to hear I had actually landed a respectable job far from the dank tombs of the Valley of the Kings she drank too much wine and spent most of the time in the ladies' room.

It was during one of her trips that Mark took my hand, looked me in the eyes, and told me he had fallen in love with someone else. Her name was Bitsy, her family was old Boston, and her money even older. He patted me on the head, said I would be fine, and was gone before Mother returned.

I wasn't fine. I was a mess. I blew off the job in Boston and instead slunk around Mother's house in my old terry cloth bathrobe and worn-out fuzzy slippers and snapped when she tried to talk to me. I couldn't stand her stiff-upper-lip-life-will-go-on attitude when mine had clearly hit the skids. I spent hours either lying in a lifeless lump on the couch or raging through the house cursing Mark in the worst language I could think of.

When I was in the couch phase, I happened to see an article about Wake Forest, North Carolina. It looked like a quaint, lovely, pastoral, peaceful place. Just what I needed. I packed up my old VW and moved there. Just like that. And it turned out to be the best decision I ever made because that's where I met the true love of my life, Tony. Life does sometimes take curious and unexpected turns.

But enough reminiscing about the past. We are about to have an exciting new adventure, and I can't wait to begin. Now Olivia and I go out to our veranda and watch as the Golden Eagle prepares to dock in Ketchikan. We have sailed from Seattle to our first port of call and are beyond excited to catch our first glimpse of an Alaskan town. We see charming wooden buildings built on stilts above the water as we watch the enormous ship maneuver into a slip, the gangway is lowered, and the first passengers disembark.

"Let's go," I say to my friend. "Don't forget your Port Pass. You can't get back onboard without it." This is a plastic card with each person's name and photo embedded in it. You do everything with this card: buy drinks, shop at the ship stores, and use it to get through security.

Olivia isn't listening. She's fiddling with her hair. "I can't do anything with this," she says. "I look awful."

She couldn't look awful if she tried—something she would never do. Her suntanned skin is flawless, her body curves in all the right places, and her hair—a mass of chestnut curls that gracefully frame her face—is perfect. But you can't tell Olivia she looks great because she won't believe you. Now she pulls on an errant strand. "This is a mess. I should have used more conditioner."

"We're on a ship," I remind her. "We're bound to get a bit windblown. And what does it matter? We don't know anyone. We could even go without makeup."

It makes me laugh to hear Olivia gasp. "I can assure you that will never happen. I don't even leave my bathroom without concealer, mascara, and blush."

I'm wearing no makeup, jeans, and a windbreaker with a hoodie, but it's raining out there, and I'm a practical person. Twenty long minutes later Olivia is satisfied with her appearance and has hidden her hair under a rain hat. We take the elevator to Deck 6 to disembark and follow the line of folks waiting patiently at the security station. Once the Port Passes are scanned into a computer, we walk down the gangway and step onto the dock. There are dark clouds swirling in the sky above our heads and a persistent rain is blowing in our faces, but nothing is going to dampen my spirits. We are in Alaska!

On the dock, throngs of people mill about trying to locate their excursion leaders. I look back at the Golden Eagle. It is enormous, and Deck 11 is very high up. I see folks on the Sport Deck and wonder how many passengers stay onboard at a port. Why would someone prefer exercise to exploring a new place? More to the point, why would anyone prefer exercise to almost anything?

"Make sure you don't lose your Port Pass. You'd better put it somewhere safe," I tell Olivia. "If you lose it, you'll have to stay in Ketchikan."

She's obviously not paying a bit of attention to what I'm saying. "I wonder what kind of shops they have here," she says. "I read in the ship's newspaper this is a good place to buy diamonds."

"Then we shall go diamond shopping." I am kidding. Together we couldn't scrape up enough money to buy a plastic one, much less a real one, but I'm not sure Olivia remembers that because she perks right up.

"I'll find the store on my map."

We don't have time for that now. We have tickets to see the totem poles, and there's our transportation."

A dusty blue van waits in a line with other vehicles. The driver, a woman dressed in a long flowered skirt, tunic-like sweater, and rain boots is standing outside the van holding a sign that says Potlatch Park and Beyond Tour. We climb in and find seats in the back. Soon several other tourists join us, the driver starts the engine, and away we go. As we jostle down the rough road, I try to wipe the steam off the windows so I can see out. The driver picks up a mic and informs us her name is Annie, she is the lunch lady at the local school in the off-season, and she is thrilled to be taking us to the park.

Olivia nudges me in the ribs and inclines her head at the seat across from us. The man sitting there reminds me of a prizefighter—muscular and solid, with a shaved, shiny head and a neck like a tree trunk.

"I know who that is," she whispers. "It's the guy in the stateroom next to us. I've seen him a couple times in the hall. I'm going to be friendly and say hi."

This doesn't surprise me. Olivia must exude some kind of exotic pheromone because men trail after her like rats following the proverbial piper. I will blame the weather for the fact that this one hasn't noticed her yet. The rain must have dampened the scent.

She unconsciously gives her rain hat a pat and leans across the aisle. "Well, hello. We're almost roommates. My friend and I have the room next to yours." She extends a beautifully manicured hand. "I'm Olivia."

Lordy! One thing about her—she ain't shy.

he man puts down the pamphlet he was reading and smiles. "Sean Mauer. And I've seen you in the hall."

he two begin to talk, and I know Olivia is trying to determine his height because she's tall and likes to wear heels. It will disappoint her if he's shorter than she is. As I listen to their chatter, I'm feeling more and more like a bag lady. I look out the window and try to pay attention to Annie, but my mind keeps drifting back to the days when I, too, had pheromones. Not as blatant as Olivia's, but I had some.

After my precipitous rush to North Carolina, I decided to go back to college at UNC. This time I wanted to study something different that wouldn't require my presence in faraway countries. Computer science seemed ideal. I'd learn a useful skill and make a ton of money using it. The fact that I could barely access my email didn't dampen my enthusiasm. But the classes did. The professor might as well have been speaking a foreign language when he talked about codes, CPU, and bit. I quickly realized computer science wasn't for me and decided to go with something I knew. I began to study for a master's degree in art history.

It was during this time I met Tony Greene, the aforementioned love of my life. He was an ex-Marine studying business, and we married as soon as he graduated. Soon after that Tony realized he didn't belong in the business world anymore than I did in the computer field. When he told me he wanted to become a cop, would probably never earn a lot of money, and would be doing dangerous work, I was all for it because I was in my let's-all-be-happy-money-doesn't-matter phase. I planned to sell marvelous but as yet unpainted masterpieces at local fairs and support us splendidly. It turned out my artistic creations weren't necessary because Tony rose to the rank of Captain, and we were doing quite nicely.

One night I called Tony and asked him to pick up some Advil on his way home from work. He stopped at a convenience store, and while he was perusing the shelves for the medication, some idiot decided to rob the place. Tony pulled out his weapon and yelled, "Put up your hands." The idiot turned and shot my wonderful husband right through the heart. One bullet. He died instantly.

This horrendous incident sent me into a tailspin from which it took forever to recover. It's been three years, and I still get tears in my eyes when I think about him or see his favorite shirt hanging in my closet or see the photo of the two of us on my bedside table. I gave up studying at UNC and pretty much everything else. If it hadn't been for my childhood friend, Olivia, I would probably still be locked in my house eating ramen noodles, crackers, and olives. She's the one who convinced me to pull up my socks and get on with life. She, too, was alone. After three failed marriages, she had decided to give up on sanctioned relationships.

Much to our surprise, we discovered we both could bake edible cakes, quiches, and cupcakes. She moved to Wake Forest, and we opened Little Bites. In the beginning, I liked it because when I was mixing flour, sugar, butter, and eggs in a bowl, my mind wasn't thinking about Tony. Now I like it because it all tastes good.

I've only been interested in one man since Tony died. I met him on a trip to Iceland, and I thought we had a real connection. I felt it from the second I met him, and I think he did, too. He was handsome and kind and smart and sometimes I still daydream about a life with him. But then I remember my daydreams about a life with Mark and how that turned out. Besides, he lives in California, and I am clear across the country so I've convinced myself I don't need anymore heartache, and there isn't much point in pursuing a long-distance relationship. Is that the right decision? I don't know. Avoiding emotional entanglement prevents emotional messes, but it isn't much fun to live alone.

Now the van bounces down a dirt road and pulls onto a grassy area, and we clamber out of our seats. Ahead of us two large colorful wooden ravens guard either side of an arch bearing the words "Potlatch Park." There are amazing totem poles everywhere. I find myself listening attentively to Annie as she describes the meaning of each pole. Some are humorous, some are memorials to commemorate someone's life, and some are meant to ridicule a wayward member of the community. I love the colors and am astounded to hear the artisans who carved these used charcoal, red pumice pebbles, and other natural materials. No going to the store and buying a tube of alizarin crimson.

Sean is turning out to be a very nice guy. He walks and talks with both of us, and his interest in Olivia seems to be purely platonic. He has an easygoing, warm personality and knows a lot about Alaska. He tells us he had looked forward to coming on this trip with his son, who had to cancel at the last minute. I know Olivia is dying to ask if he's married but wisely refrains. I also know she isn't paying attention when he talks about the history of Ketchikan.

"Imagine people passed through this area 12,000 years ago, and some settled here because the weather was cool and there were lots of fish. And rain. Did you know Ketchikan gets 162 inches of rain a year?" He looks sheepish. "I must admit I'm a bit of a history geek."

"The totem poles are masterpieces," I say. "It's amazing to think they used natural pigments to achieve such vibrant colors—colors that have lasted all these years."

Sean agrees. "I know of several artists who use only natural colors, and they produce beautiful pieces of art."

I'd like to talk more about this, but I can see our conversation is beginning to bore Olivia. She is my wonderful, amazing friend, but she doesn't travel to new places to explore the history and culture. Her interests are primarily centered around retail establishments. She can tell you where to buy diamonds, wool sweaters, silver jewelry, and just about anything else in every city she visits, and her eyes glaze over quickly when the talk turns to history, art museums, and local lore. Since I hate to shop, love art museums, and am fascinated by history, we balance each other nicely. Our common denominator is food.

When she persuades Sean to visit the gift shop with her, I follow Annie into a clan house. The first thing I see is a marvelous carved eagle on the wall. Its wings are spread, and the body is embellished with a brilliant turquoise. I am so engrossed in studying the wonderful piece of art, I don't realize Annie and the others have left, and I am alone until the door slams shut, suddenly plunging the room into near darkness. Too late I remember Annie telling us to keep the door open since there's no electricity. There's a sliver of light coming through a partially shuttered window. The totem poles I had considered beautiful a minute ago now loom over me as black and forbidding creatures. I feel my heart lurch as I see a sudden movement to my right, and I make out two figures standing very still at the back of the house. They aren't totem poles because I can hear soft whispers.

I try my voice, but it doesn't seem to be working. This is ridiculous, I tell myself. There's nothing to be afraid of. Your imagination is working overtime. Get a grip. Walk to the door and get out of here. But my feet don't seem to be working either, and worse, the two figures that were motionless a minute ago, are now coming toward me.

I turn around and bang into a protuberance on a totem pole. Whatever it is jabs me in the stomach, and I almost scream. I am willing myself not to pass out when the door flies open and Olivia bursts into the house.

"There you are! We've been looking all over for you. Annie says it's time to go."

Thank heavens! I pull myself together and step outside. Daylight chases the goblins away, and I quickly join the others for the drive to town. Annie parks the van and hands us a map.

"I've marked all the shops that won't rip you off. There are some that will try, so be careful." She points to a series of houses built on wooden boardwalks. "Make sure you go to Creek Street. And look down at the water. The salmon are all coming back from the ocean to spawn in their birthplace, and you'll be able to see tons of them."

Within minutes Olivia spies sweaters in a boutique window and disappears into the shop. Sean and I keep walking. As we chat, I know Olivia is going to be disappointed, and she can save her false eyelashes for another occasion because Sean doesn't behave like a man looking for willing women—even one as alluring as Olivia. He's excited about being in Alaska, is looking forward to excursions in other cities, and actually goes to the wildlife lectures offered onboard the ship.

He pulls out his phone and shows me amazing photos he's taken of eagles soaring in the sky and whales breaching. He points to a picture of an eagle sitting on a piling at the dock and says, "These birds are incredible. I know I was gawking like a tourist when I took this, but it isn't an everyday sight for me."

I nod. "When I lived in South Carolina, it always amazed me to see people staring at the alligators. We saw them all the time. Tourists ran down to the water to take photos. Smart natives stayed away."

We soon discover we have a common interest in art beyond totem poles. He tells me about visiting the Musée d'Orsay in Paris and being awestruck at the Impressionist paintings. That's one of my favorite periods, too, so we talk about Monet, Manet and Pisarro. I find myself telling him about my art degree from Columbia and my almost master's degree. When he asks why I didn't finish, I almost tell him. But I don't, and he doesn't press me.

We walk for a bit in silence, and then he says, "I wanted to be a sculptor. I loved the satisfaction of molding something out of a hunk of clay." He laughs. "But reality had to prevail. I had a scholarship to college, and the business school didn't offer sculpting classes. And my parents thought I'd be a pauper if I tried a career as an artist." He pauses. "Things turned out for the best. I'm very happy, and I can always visit a gallery if I need a fix."

By now we've walked past all the shops and are waiting for Olivia. She appears with two bags and a smile on her face. "I found excellent buys. These sweaters will be great in the winter." She pulls out a thick blue pullover that looks itchy and very hot.

"We live in North Carolina," I tell her. "That looks suitable for Arctic wear."

"Nonsense. It will be great for walking the dogs."

"You don't have dogs."

"No, but you do. I can help."

"Whatever." I shrug and glance at Sean, who is smiling.

"I'm sending some smoked salmon to my family back home," he says. "I know you can buy it there, but getting it right from the source will be special. I'm also ready for a beer. Want to join me?"

I can see Olivia is torn, but more shopping wins. She shakes her head. "No, thanks, but we'd take you up on a drink later onboard the ship."

"You've got it. How about 5:30 at that bar on the top deck? It's nice to sit outside, and last night it wasn't crowded."

"That would be perfect," Olivia says gaily. He is already forgotten as she consults her map and links elbows with me. "First we'll hit the art stores because I know you like them, and then let's do a little jewelry shopping."

As we walk away, I see Sean stop to talk to a man. Our new friend appears upset, and I'm hoping he doesn't do anything stupid like take a swing at the guy because the man is considerably taller and bigger than Sean.

Two hours later, we have purchased a tiny totem pole, three bangle bracelets—pretty, but of dubious material—and a pound of chocolate truffles. When Olivia says, "Let's go back to the ship and have some lunch." I'm all for it. I don't like shopping and I do like food.

CHAPTER TWO

"I can't understand why he didn't show up. I'm sure he said 5:30," Olivia says as she looks around the lounge. It's 6:15 and we're sitting by ourselves drinking wine. Sean isn't here.

"I don't know," I tell her. "Maybe he found something else to do in town." But secretly, I'm surprised. He and I had such a nice conversation, and I'd really looked forward to talking to him again.

Olivia looks doubtful. "Maybe. It just seems odd. And he has to be back. We've already sailed." This is true. From our vantage point we can see the buildings on Ketchikan become smaller and smaller.

I notice that Olivia has taken particular care with her appearance this evening. She's wearing a lavender flowing creation that drapes around her body perfectly. Her hair is swept up and held in place with a butterfly clip. There is glitter on her eyelids.

"You look really nice," I tell her, "but I don't think Sean is looking for anything but a pleasant trip."

She applies more rose lip gloss and says, "You can't know that. He's an extremely interesting man. I do like it when they're smart. And he has a great sense of humor."

Lordy! "I think he's exactly what he seems to be—a nice guy excited about a trip to Alaska. He doesn't behave like a man who wants to hook up with a stranger."

And it's obvious he isn't coming, but we wait until 6:30 and then make our way to the Trattoria Italiana. As the maître d' leads us to our table, I whisper to Olivia, "I am so happy we chose Anytime Dining. This is way better than sitting in the huge main dining room." The place smells wonderful, and I love the décor: photos of sun-drenched Tuscan vineyards nicely placed on red walls and tables with white cloths and full bottles of wine in the center.

We are seated at a table for four, and the other two are already there. A pleasant-looking woman with a round, cheerful face, red lipstick, and shoulder-length brown hair puts down her glass of wine and extends her hand. "Hi. I'm Melissa Andrews, and this is my sister, Tina." The woman next to her puts two fingers to her forehead in a salute. "Nice to meet you." We introduce ourselves.

Tina has thin mousy blonde hair that she wears absolutely straight, which is unfortunate because her forehead is high and needs a little something in the way of camouflage. She also doesn't smile as readily as her sister.

Before we get into the small talk, we study the menu, and Olivia and I both decide on caprese salads, a shrimp and pasta dish, and a nice pinot grigio. When the wine comes, I settle back in my chair, prepared for the inevitable, "Where are you from?"

"So where are you from?" Melissa asks. Without waiting for an answer, she offers more information. "We're teachers from Ohio. I teach fourth grade. Tina is a professor in Animal Breeding and Genetics, but she's on a sabbatical now. What do you gals do?"

I hate being called a gal, so I clamp my mouth shut. Aware of this, Olivia tries to fill the awkward silence. "I'm Olivia Duncan, and this is Julia Greene. We have a little business in North Carolina. Is this your first trip to Alaska?"

"Sure is." Melissa smears butter on a breadstick. "You know, I think you gals are on our deck. Deck 11? I like to read those little name cards in the slots on the doors, and I remember seeing yours."

The food makes a fortuitous arrival, and for a few minutes we are silent as we dig in. The caprese salad is excellent—there are generous globs of tasty burrata cheese—and I eye Olivia's plate, hoping she deems it too calorific to eat. But no such luck. She devours it as fast as I do. Honestly, it's so good I wish I could lick up the remains of the olive oil, garlic, and balsamic vinegar dressing.

When I see Tina put down her fork and look at us, I try to smile politely. She finally speaks, "What is your opinion of lemurs?"

Excuse me? I think for a minute I haven't heard her correctly. "Did you say lemurs? Do you mean those monkey-like creatures?"

Tina bristles. "They are decidedly not monkeys. People always make that mistake. Have you ever been to Madagascar?"

Olivia laughs. "I don't even know where that is. Julia doesn't either."

Melissa finishes her beef with noodles and pushes the plate away. "My sister keeps lemurs in our basement. She studies their behavior for the university."

"How very fascinating." These women are quite possibly not playing with a full deck, and I wish I were anywhere but here. This is the reason I hate sharing tables with strangers. Call me antisocial but I hate small talk, and right now I'd rather be sharing pizza in our room with a lemur than chatting with these ladies. I look at Olivia for help.

She, thankfully, changes the subject. "Where do you live in Ohio? I'm sort of familiar with the state."

"You probably wouldn't know it," Melissa assures us. "It's a little town called Bath."

Olivia claps her hands. "Well, for heaven's sake, I do. My friend works in the elementary school. Florence Rogers. You must know her. She teaches fifth grade."

"I sure do. Great gal. I'll be sure to say hello when I get home."

Olivia is about to reply when the loudspeaker crackles to life. The voice is so heavily accented, it's difficult to figure out what it's saying.

"Buona sera, signore e signori. Scusa. Here is Capitano Bianchi. We ave de reports of de murder on Deck 9. First-stage response team is there now. We also investigating supicious smale in passenger pantry."

Olivia puts down her fork. "What did he just say? They've sent a first response team to investigate a murder? I mean, the captain is hard to understand, but that sounds exactly like what he said. And a 'supicious smale'? Could he have meant suspicious male?"

To say Captain Antonio Bianchi is difficult to understand is an understatement. He may be a first-class boat captain, but his English is almost nonexistent. And judging from the rising murmur in the restaurant, we aren't the only ones who are puzzled. A man at the table next to us leans over and says, "Sounds like we have a crime onboard. This sure isn't what I paid for."

"Me neither." Olivia's voice is too loud, but no one seems to notice. "I'm not staying on this ship with a murderer."

I try to calm my friend down. "It would be a bit difficult to get off. As you pointed out earlier, we left Ketchikan a few hours ago. Maybe this is one of those mystery games people play. You know, someone is killed, and the rest of the passengers have to figure out who did it."

Olivia looks doubtful. "There wasn't anything about it in the ship's daily newspaper. Seems to me they would warn people."

"I don't think they would," I say as I attempt to resume eating. "I'm sure there's nothing wrong." But I'm actually not so sure. I've been glancing out the window behind Olivia, and now I'm pretty certain we aren't moving. The mountain peak in the distance remains stationary, no matter how hard I stare at it.

"I don't mean to alarm you," I say in a low voice, "but take a look. I think the ship has stopped."

I guess my voice isn't low enough because four diners leave their table and rush to the window. As they talk excitedly to each other, I snag a waiter carrying a platter of food. "We've stopped. Do you know why?"

He glances briefly out the window. "We're moving. I can assure you we never stop, madam, even if there is a fire."

I look again. Same mountain peak exactly where I left it. "I'm pretty sure we're not. Do you suppose you could find out why?"

"Certainly." He doesn't look happy, but he disappears in the direction of the deck and is back before I can sit down. "We're moving. I looked. Nothing to worry about. Would you care to see the dessert menu?"

"No, thank you." I look helplessly at Olivia. "Am I crazy?"

She shakes her head. "If you are, I am, too. This ship is definitely not moving."

The waiter overhears us. "Is this your first time to travel, madam? Perhaps the first time on a ship? I can promise you nothing is wrong." He lowers his voice. "You seem to be upsetting the other guests."

"The other guests aren't paying any attention to us," I snap. "And no, this is not my first time on a cruise." It's my second, but he doesn't need to know that. And it will do no good to say I know what I saw because obviously I didn't see what I thought I saw even though I know I did. And as I look out the window, the mountain peak that had been stationary is now off to the right. We are moving.

The loudspeaker blares again.

"Scusa, once more, signore e signori. This is again your Capitano. We ave found de problem. Il primo team di risposta is standing down. Buona serata. Ave a nice evening. Ciao!"

"What on earth does that mean?" Olivia mutters. "I'm very confused."

Melissa puts her napkin on the table and picks up her purse. "I'm sure it was nothing. You gals sure do panic easily." She nods at Tina, who obediently stands up and follows her sister. "See you later. I'm going to bed and read. Tomorrow we visit Juneau."

Yes, we will, I think to myself as they depart. *But first I'm going to visit Deck 9.*

CHAPTER THREE

We can't go to Deck 9 right away because as we come out of the restaurant there are many people milling about, talking about the captain's words, and there are long lines for all the elevators. Melissa, who has not gone to bed, spots us and insists we greet her two new friends. "Come meet Phoebe and Martin Skofield. They're on our deck, too. We were just talking about all the excitement in the dining room."

Phoebe extends her hand. "Hi. We thought the captain said murder, too. We were in one of the shops on the Promenade Deck. There was a short burst of panic. Several passengers were extremely upset." She has shoulder-length, curly dark blonde hair, a puff of curly bangs over her forehead, and a voice that chirps like a bird. The mass of hair dwarfs her long, pale face.

"I still think something peculiar is going on," her husband, Martin, says. "And whatever it is must be serious enough to cause the captain to make that announcement." He runs his hand through his hair. "I've asked some of the crew, but they won't tell you anything."

"Did you guys notice the ship stopped?" I have to ask—just to convince myself I saw what I saw.

Phoebe claps her hands. "I did, I did. I asked one of the ship's officers, but he said no way." She leans in close to me. "I heard they took a body off, and the person didn't die from natural causes."

This is probably wild gossip, but nevertheless fascinating. I have to hear more. "Who told you that?"

"One of the cabin stewards. I think his name is Sergio." She jerks her thumb toward her husband. "Martin gave him a drink in our room after dinner."

I must have raised my eyebrows because she says, "Hey, we have a right to know what's going on. He told Martin the first response team was down on Deck 4." She waits for me to react, and when I don't, says, "The deck with the gangway. They were using it to remove the body."

Her husband shakes his head. "I think you're wrong, sweetie. They wouldn't put the gangway out. Too many people would see that. They probably discreetly lowered the body into a tender and took it ashore."

This theory has a few holes in it. They can't have taken a body ashore in a tender because we aren't near a shore. We sailed four hours ago. And Deck 4 isn't the only deck with a gangway. But Deck 4 is the deck with the ship's hospital. Was someone taken there? We have enough speculation swirling around so I say, "Maybe there isn't a body. I'm pretty sure the captain wouldn't announce a crime over the loudspeaker. That could cause a panic."

Phoebe seems disappointed. "There has to have been something. They wouldn't call out the first response team if there wasn't a problem."

She is probably right.

Olivia and I say goodbye to the folks and stroll around the deck waiting for the line to the elevator to clear. Finally, we jump in one and push the button for 9.

"I still don't get what we're doing," she says. "Why do you want to go down there?"

"Aren't you the least bit curious?" I ask her. "Obviously something happened, and I want to see what it is."

We have to quit talking because the elevator stops at 10, and three people get on. They, too, are discussing the captain's strange remarks. A tall man with a florid face, no hair, and an impressive waistline turns to me. "Did you hear him? I thought he said there was a murder. I told my wife we needed to call the authorities and get this ship stopped."

The wife, a short, tired-looking lady with gray hair, nods. "I think it's a disgrace to have a crime on a cruise like this. I couldn't get a cell phone signal, but I'll bet others tried to report it."

"The captain's English isn't very good. I've been thinking about it. Maybe he was trying to say they were investigating a suspicious odor, not murder. And I think maybe the ship was stopped," I offer. "At least it didn't seem to be moving for a while."

"Really? Didn't notice that. We were in the Pelican Lounge having after-dinner drinks. But tell me this— why would a first response team investigate an odor? That doesn't make much sense."

He makes a good point. I have no idea.

The elevator glides to a stop on Deck 9. The door opens, and I hold my breath waiting to see if the others get off. They don't. We step out, they wish us goodnight, the door closes, and we are alone.

"So now what?" Olivia asks. "It feels spooky down here."

"Nonsense." But it does. And the notice posted next to the elevator doesn't help.

ALL ROOMS ON THE PORT SIDE OF THE SHIP WILL BE SUBJECTED TO VIGOROUS DISINFECTION. PLEASE DO NOT USE YOUR ROOM UNTIL INFORMED BY THE FRONT DESK.

This makes no sense, and I wonder what the problem is in the rooms. I walk briskly across the ornately patterned maroon rug and consult the floor directory. "It seems there are only staterooms on this deck.

Staterooms and a self-service laundry." I sniff the air like a bloodhound searching for a scent. "Do you smell that? It smells like something from the sewer mixed with some kind of bleach or cleaning product."

Olivia holds her nose. "Maybe toilets are backed up. I know that often happens on cruises."

"That's not what it smells like. It's much more pungent."

I know we're supposed to stay away from this side of the ship, but I start walking down a long hall on the port side. "What do you suppose is a passenger pantry?"

Olivia giggles. "Maybe a place with shelves and pillows and stuff—for passengers on a budget. That would really be low-cost cruising."

My mind instantly conjures up images of drawers stuffed with people looking for discounted fares. "It would, indeed," I tell her, "but it's probably more like a supply closet with things the room stewards might need. And the 'supicious smale' might not be a suspicious male at all. More likely the captain was trying to say smell."

"That all sounds terribly innocent. And boring. So why are we down here?"

"Because the ship did stop," I tell her, "no matter what the dining room steward said. And something was serious enough to cause the captain to make that announcement. I would just like to know what it was. I was a cop's wife, so I've learned how to spot trouble."

Olivia rolls her eyes but is smart enough not to reply.

By now we have walked the entire length of the hall and encountered absolutely no one. Ahead is the self-service laundry. Someone has obviously tried to get rid of the unpleasant odor, but it is stronger in here. There are two washers, two dryers, some ironing boards and a token machine, and a machine that dispenses small boxes of detergent.

Olivia taps the glass door with her fingernail. "We should leave, but first I need some soap to wash my undies. How do we do this?"

It takes two of us to figure out how to swipe our Port Pass to buy tokens. Olivia inserts the token into the soap machine and tries to push the lever. "It won't go," she says. "It feels like something is stuck in there." She gets down on her knees and sticks her fingers into the machine. "I can feel it. Hand me that coat hanger." She quickly bends it into a hook and fishes around. "Almost have it. It's not very big, but it's blocking the soap boxes. Ah ha!"

She pulls out the hanger and along with it a piece of fabric. "How in the world did that get in there?" She has a fragment of yellow cloth in her hand.

"It looks like the remains of a pocket," I tell her, "and there's something in there."

With thumb and index finger, she removes a piece of plastic and hands it to me. "What do you make of that?"

"It's part of someone's Port Pass," I say. "You can see Golden E and part of the date 08/14, so it belongs to someone on this trip. And look here. Do you see the name Sean Ma...? Isn't that the name of our friend in the stateroom next to ours? The one who was supposed to meet us for drinks?"

"So that means he's back on the ship," Olivia says.

I turn the Pass over and see something dark red on the back. "It looks that way, but I would think he would be missing this card."

"Maybe he got a new one at the front desk. I've seen people do that. What is that?" she asks, poking at the red spot. "Is it ketchup?"

"Or blood," I say. "Don't touch it." This is giving me a very bad feeling. Why would a piece of possibly bloody fabric be stuffed in the detergent vending machine slot?

"Let's go to his cabin and tell him we found this," Olivia says. "He may not know he lost it."

I wish with all my heart I could be as naïve as Olivia. We can probably assume he didn't tear his shirt himself and then dispose of the piece of material in the laundry room. That means someone else did. And we can also probably assume the tearing didn't happen accidentally because why would someone hide this if Sean had innocently fallen or hurt himself on something jagged? So the only logical conclusion is Sean has been hurt and is in some kind of trouble—or worse. I trudge behind Olivia, desperately hoping I am wrong.

It's still light outside, and Olivia and I are back out on deck because after our jaunt to Deck 9 I'm not the least bit sleepy. The late evening sun makes the water glow a warm orange. We walk to the railing and watch a pod of whales cavort in the ocean. Occasionally, they blow geysers of water and then throw their flukes high into the air before they dive. "They look like they're playing," I say to my friend. "This is incredible."

We are alone on this section of the deck—except for a woman standing a short distance from us. Now she approaches us smiling. "Rebecca MacPherson," she says as she sticks out her hand. "I'm the naturalist onboard. I'm supposed to be telling people all about the whales and wild life, but look around. Do you see anyone else out here enjoying this wonderful sight?" She pushes an errant clump of thick white hair out of her face. "They complain about not seeing whales, but I'll bet they are all in there playing bingo or something. Why come to Alaska if you don't want to see all these wonderful creatures?" As if to prove her point, a whale breaches in front of our eyes—its fin smacking the water. "See what I mean? That is awesome, and we're the only ones watching." Her bright blue eyes sparkle.

"I love talking about whales and eagles and everything. You'd think the passengers would, too."

I instantly like this no-nonsense woman. Dressed in khaki slacks and a green windbreaker she is the perfect outdoor Alaskan. She points to a group of trees off to the left. "If you stay out here a few more minutes, I'll show you a wonderful eagle's nest. It's too bad we're not on the top deck because we would have a better view, but we'll be past the spot by the time we race up there." She chuckles. "Last night I was out here quite late looking at the gorgeous moon, and I saw two idiots climbing down from a lifeboat. It was too dark to see if they were men, women, or a combination, but they had no business being up there. When they saw me, they ran down the deck to the bow. Like I said. Idiots."

Olivia smiles. "Maybe two people looking for a private spot?"

Rebecca shakes her head. "That's what cabins are for. Lifeboats are off limits to passengers. First of all, it's dangerous to climb there, and I'm pretty sure you can't get in. Look!" she yells. "There's the nest. And there's an eagle carrying a fish. Can you get a picture?"

I use my cell phone camera to follow the magnificent bird as it soars across the sky. I've taken about a bazillion pictures since we left Seattle but haven't found time to sort them.

"We're in Frederick Sound now, so we should be seeing some humpbacks. After I give my spiel over the loudspeaker, which probably no one will listen to, I'd be happy to tell you more about these wonderful whales. We could meet here around sometime tomorrow."

"We'll be here," I assure her. "This is the most awesome scenery I've ever seen." I pause. As I chat with Rebecca, I try to work up courage to ask her a question. She works on the ship so she would know all the gossip. Maybe she has heard something about Sean.

"Say, you haven't heard anything about a missing passenger, have you?"

She eyes me curiously. "Sure haven't. Why do you ask that?"

I shrug. "I haven't seen a friend for a while—well, not exactly a friend, but someone I met. The three of us were going to have drinks together, and he never showed up." And since I don't seem to know when to stop talking, I say, "There was that funny incident with the captain's announcement and first response team and such, and I just wondered if something has happened."

"Not that I know of. I did hear the captain make that announcement and thought it was strange. His English isn't very good. Haven't heard anything about a missing passenger, though, and I'm pretty sure I would have. The crew likes to gossip. Got to run now, folks. I'm due to give a little talk about glaciers in the Sand and Sea Lounge."

"See," Olivia says as our new friend walks away. "Nothing suspicious. You have to put that overactive imagination to sleep."

I wish I could, but that ripped Port Pass didn't bloody itself.

As we head back to our cabin, we meet the room steward carrying a load of towels. He smiles, and I smile back, then stop and call after him. "Excuse me, could I ask you a question? We're looking for the man in the cabin next to ours. We haven't seen him since Ketchikan, and my friend and I are worried."

He lowers his eyes, and I'm sure he thinks I'm one of the females stalking male passengers.

"No, madam, I have not seen him. I keep his room clean. He perhaps...ah...somewhere else on the ship?"

I know he's trying to be discreet, so I change direction. "You must know everything that happens. Would it be possible for a passenger to jump overboard without being noticed?"

He looks alarmed, but nevertheless answers politely. His English is limited, but he does his best. "No, madam, no one jump without being seen. There are big security cameras everywhere." He spreads his arms wide open. "They see everything—all the deck at once."

"Everywhere on the ship?"

"Yes. Maybe no. Maybe not crew quarter everywhere."

This is good to know. Sean came back to the Golden Eagle and didn't go overboard. He is here somewhere.

CHAPTER FOUR

As we approach our room, we meet the Andrews sisters coming out of theirs. "Told you we have cabins close to each other," Melissa says gaily. "Just one room between us." And that stateroom happens to belong to our missing friend, Sean. "We decided we can sleep when we're home, so we're on our way to the theater to watch the show. Want to come?"

I shake my head. "No, thanks. We're looking for the guy in this cabin." I point to Sean's. "You haven't happened to have seen him, have you?"

Tina finally speaks. "There's probably no point in looking for him. We saw him in Ketchikan. I think he said he was going to stay there for a while. Maybe he plans to catch up with the ship in Skagway."

"But that's not possible," Olivia begins. "We found…" I stop her by stepping hard on her foot. No need to mention the piece of torn shirt or the ripped Port Pass.

Fortunately, Melissa doesn't seem to have heard her.

"Well, if he isn't onboard, I'm glad the ship didn't wait. There are always a few people who think they're special and ignore departure time. The captain is right to leave without them."

As she talks, I study the sisters. They must have either a different mother or father because they sure don't resemble each other. Melissa reminds me of a sturdy tree—tall and strong. Tina is about five feet tall and can't possibly weigh more than 100 pounds, and she doesn't look like she's strong enough to pick up a book.

But this isn't the time to examine the physical attributes of these ladies, and, to be perfectly honest, I don't really care. I want them to leave so we can knock on Sean's door.

I make a pretense of hunting through my purse until I see them step into an elevator at the end of the hall. Then I zoom over to Sean's room and rap lightly. When there's no response—and I'm really not expecting one—I knock harder.

Olivia has the door to our room open. "He's not there. Come in before you make other passengers curious."

Once inside we kick off our shoes. Our beds have been turned down for the night, and there are chocolate mints on the pillows, but we're not yet ready for sleep. Olivia brings a bottle of chardonnay and two glasses to the veranda where we settle ourselves into chairs and watch lights from the ship bounce off the water as we slide through the dark night.

"Something isn't right," I say to Olivia. "Sean has to have come back onboard. How else can we explain the torn Port Pass? Something has happened to him."

I feel Olivia shudder. "You're scaring me a bit. I think the captain's announcement has put your imagination into overdrive. Sean is probably with some woman. I noticed there are a lot of them trolling on this ship."

Maybe, and I want to believe that, but it still doesn't explain the torn piece of fabric. I'm so antsy I can't sit still, so I get up and pace around the small veranda. "It really is bugging me not knowing where he is. I'm worried something has happened to him."

"For heaven's sake, Julia, let it go. Why do you care? Maybe he's in the casino or with a bimbo in her cabin, or, I don't know, drunk in a bar someplace. Besides, Tina said he stayed in Ketchikan." I'm about to speak, but she puts up her hand. "I know—the torn Port Pass. I can't explain how it came to be stuck in a soap dispenser, but there must be a very logical explanation."

I get to my feet and try to peer around the partition dividing the staterooms. It's difficult to see anything because they were designed to provide privacy. At least I'm able to see there is no light coming from the room.

I give up and turn back to Olivia. "How can there possibly be a rational explanation for stuffing fabric up a slot? I'm thinking there must be a way to find out if Sean is onboard." I pull the torn Port Pass out of my pocket. "The part you stick into the lock is still intact. I'll bet I can use it to get into his room."

"You really are crazy. What if you get caught or a room steward sees you? Or even worse, what if Sean is in there with a woman and doesn't want to be disturbed?"

But I am beyond rational thought. "Just a quick look," I tell my friend. "I'll be back in a flash. And you can keep a lookout in the hall—just in case."

Olivia vigorously shakes her head, but I'm out the door before she can tell me I'm nuts.

I knock softly and sing one verse of 'Old MacDonald Had a Farm' to myself as I wait for the door to fly open and an angry Sean to burst out. When that doesn't happen, I hold my breath and insert the torn card. Miracle of miracles, it slides into the lock and the green light indicates the door is open. My heart is pounding like a jackhammer as I creep into the room and close the door. I turn on the flashlight on my cell phone and shine it around the cabin.

The bed is neatly made and obviously hasn't been slept in. And there is absolute proof Sean has come back to the ship. A lightweight blue jacket—the one I remember seeing him wear in Ketchikan—hangs on the back of a chair. There are two identical small bags on the table, each with a Ketchikan gift shop logo. Inside are pretty bracelets and necklaces made from brightly colored stones. They look like something little girls would love.

Next to his bed there is a small framed photo of Sean with his arm around a pretty woman with red hair. Two little girls stand in front of them eating chocolate ice cream cones. The girls have chocolate smeared on their faces, and all four are laughing. They look so happy. Sean in the photo doesn't look like the sort of man who would be prowling for other women. I know—looks can be deceiving, but he looks like a man who is happily married and loves his kids.

I pick up a copy of *Alexander Hamilton* that is open, face down on the table. The top corner of page 113 is turned down. Was Sean reading when someone interrupted him? He must have gone willingly because there's no sign of a struggle.

I'm about to leave when something catches my eye. On the side of the chair, almost stuck under the cushion is his cell phone. This really alarms me. No one goes anywhere without his phone. We're all so attached to out electronic gadgets, it's impossible to think Sean would decide to get a beer or food and leave his phone behind. As to what happens next—I can only say the devil made me do it. I stick the phone in my pocket and head to the door.

I'm about to step into the hall when I hear voices. One is very loud and belongs to Olivia. "It's so early," she says. "We can sleep when we're home. Come on, I'll buy you a drink." Bless her. She's trying to lure the ladies away from Sean's room.

A testy Melissa isn't interested. "No, thanks. The show wasn't very good, and I'm ready for bed."

"I hear they have wonderful margaritas in that lounge on the Promenade Deck. Doesn't that sound good?" Olivia is trying, but the ladies aren't interested.

"Frankly, from what I've seen, I think you and your friend drink too much. Now could you please step aside? You're blocking our room."

When I hear a door bang, I assume the ladies have declined Olivia's invitation. Inside their room, they turn on a light, which illuminates the veranda next door. I creep to the veranda door in Sean's room and carefully open it a few inches. Melissa and Tina are standing outside and talking softly. I catch snatches of Skagway and something about a phone call that has to be made tomorrow. Melissa seems to be scolding Tina for being a "silly little twit." Tina seems so colorless, it's hard to imagine her being silly or a twit, but it's good to know she has it in her. Melissa is obviously the older, bossy sister. I can't hear anything Tina is saying.

I don't close the veranda door until Melissa's voice fades as the two go back inside. The heavy door makes a noise as I push it shut, and I hold my breath waiting for the ladies to start yelling. I have to get out of here right now, so I text Olivia on my cell phone.

Me: I'm coming out, and the door makes a loud noise when it closes. Can you create a diversion?

O: What would that be? I told you not to do this. I don't know how you're going to close the door without them hearing.

Me: If you open our door, I'll close this one as quietly as I can and then run into our room. It has to be simultaneous.

But it turns out our plan isn't necessary. Just as I'm about to open Sean's door, I hear the ladies' door open and then close. Melissa and Tina seem to be on the move. I step into the hall in time to see their backs retreating toward the elevators.

By the time I wash my face and get ready for bed, I am completely exhausted. All this mystery has wiped me out. I'm not too tired, however, to have a look at Sean's cell phone. I turn it over in my hand, hoping it will miraculously divulge some clue about his whereabouts. But no such luck. It's locked, and I have no idea how to discover the code. I toss the phone into the first thing I see, which happens to be my gold Lamé evening bag lying on top of my open suitcase.

CHAPTER FIVE

The ship has stopped. I can say this with certainty because it's daylight and I can see clearly. I am out on the veranda and watch as a small boat comes along side and a person jumps from the boat onto our ship.

There's also an alarming commotion coming from somewhere below. I throw on my jacket and dash out the door, and the first person I see on deck is Melissa, who's so upset I can hardly understand what she's saying.

"It's just so terrible. I mean, how can something like this happen? Tina is so distraught she had to lie down. Come on. We have to go see."

"See what? I'm not going anywhere until you tell me what's going on."

She wrings her hands, then nervously tries to jam them in her pockets. "It's awful. They found a body—and in the strangest place."

I'm slow to comprehend, but when I do, a sick feeling rushes to my stomach. "You mean a dead person? Do they know who it is? Was it a man?"

"I think so. He jumped from the top deck but apparently didn't judge his distance correctly because instead of landing in the water, he landed on top of a lifeboat. So terrible. It's a good thing we're close to Juneau. I'm sure they'll take the body off there."

Fear lurches in my stomach. "Who is it? Is it a passenger?

"I don't know if it's a passenger, but I think I heard it's a man. I also heard there was blood everywhere.

Pity the poor folks who were out on deck and discovered him."

I want to say we should pity the poor soul who jumped, but I don't want to talk to Melissa anymore. I want to find out the identity of the dead person and make sure it isn't Sean. And I think I have a way to find out.

I spot Rebecca MacPherson leaning on the rail in the bow of the ship. When she sees me, she says, "No one is interested in wildlife right now. They're all chattering about the dead man."

So it is a man! I'm not quite sure how to phrase my next question. I decide the best way is to plunge right in. "That's actually why I want to talk to you. Do you happen to know if he was a passenger?"

She gives me a funny look. "I have no idea. No one is saying. They took the body away pretty quickly."

"I hate to sound ghoulish," I say, "but what do they do with a body on a cruise ship? Is there a morgue or something?"

She nods. "Most large ships have a designated morgue. They hold the body there until the ship reaches a port. We dock soon in Juneau, and I suspect the body will be taken there. Or maybe they'll keep it onboard until we reach Seattle. Sometimes they do that because of all the paperwork." She hesitates. "I feel sorry for his family. Imagine cheerfully waving goodbye to your loved one only to have him come back dead."

I gulp. In my mind, I'm seeing the photo of the smiling woman and little girls. How awful for them if the dead man is Sean. "Where on a ship would this morgue be?"

"I believe it's down by the infirmary, but I'm not sure. Why are you asking these questions? You're not going to try to find it, are you?"

My laugh sounds hollow even to my ears. "Ha ha, for heaven's sake, no! That would be creepy."

But that's exactly what I'm planning to do just as soon as I can politely get away from Rebecca MacPherson.

Olivia isn't totally enthusiastic about my plan. In fact, she's adamantly against it. She looks up from applying green polish to her toenails and says, "No way I'm hunting for a body. What's wrong with you lately? Why are you so obsessed with a man we hardly know? I'm thinking you either need some kind of medication or an exorcism. Can't you just enjoy this trip without creating drama?"

I sit down next to her and try to explain. "I honestly don't know why, Olivia. Maybe it's the photo of the smiling family and the thought of their grief if Sean doesn't come home. And he and I had such a great chat about art. He was so nice and friendly and, well, happy when we saw him. Or maybe it's the suspicion something bad has happened to him. I pray I'm wrong about that, but I know either he or his body is on this ship. In any event, I have to find the answers."

I take the elevator to Deck 4. I'm down here because I have Googled morgues on ships and now believe the morgue is actually somewhere within the infirmary. The infirmaries on ships this size are quite large, so it makes sense. Store the bodies where they can keep track of them. It wouldn't do to have a wandering passenger accidentally open a door and …oops.

It's eerily quiet down here. There are no staterooms and no people. I'll have to invent an illness, but it shouldn't be difficult to convince a nurse I'm sick. My heart is pounding, and I feel like I'm going to throw up. I take a deep breath and open the door of the infirmary.

The waiting room is painted a blinding white—white couches and walls. The only color comes from a posted notice in bold red letters that says PLEASE TELL THE NURSE IMMEDIATELY IF YOU HAVE SYMPTOMS OF STOMACH FLU.

There doesn't seem to be anyone around. I timidly call out, "Hello," and when no one answers, I shout, "Is anyone here?" Still nothing. I peer behind the reception window and see the chair is empty and so is the room beyond. Maybe the entire medical staff is out on the deck attending to upset passengers.

I'm surprised the infirmary isn't bigger. There's a reception and waiting area, a hall with two examination rooms, a pharmacy, a supply room, and another room with x-ray equipment. That's it. Google is wrong. There is no morgue here.

Not willing to give up, I go behind the glass window at the reception desk and into an area with file cabinets, a computer, and a wall mount with keys. The keys are all neatly labeled. And there's one marked Morgue. How easy is that! I put it in my pocket, move quickly across the waiting area, out the door and into the hall.

I'd be willing to bet the morgue is around here somewhere, and since there are no staterooms this should be fairly easy. I count in all six doors in the hall. All I have to do is try the key in each door. Aware that people could be arriving at any moment, I try to hurry, but my hand is shaking so badly I'm having a hard time getting the key in the first lock. It doesn't turn, so I move to the second and try again.

When it doesn't work and I hear voices, I run to the stairs, go down half a flight, and crouch in the stairwell. My mind is trying to tell me this is one of the dumbest things I've ever done, but I'm not listening to my mind. I hear the elevator chime indicating it has reached this deck, and I wait until I hear no more voices, then cautiously climb back up and creep down the hall.

The key turns the lock on the third door, and I step into a cold, dark room. I use the flashlight on my phone to look around. There are three metal drawers, and I've watched enough TV to know what they're for. They hold dead bodies. But I don't have to open one because in front of the drawers is a table with a body bag. And the bag isn't empty.

Willing myself not to throw up, I try to unzip the top of the bag, but my fingers are so icy cold I can't make them work. And rational thought is trying to worm its way into my head. What am I thinking? I can't do this. I need medication!

Pushing these thoughts away, I straighten up, close my eyes, rub my hands together hard enough to start a friction fire, and get to work. I intend to open my eyes, take a quick peek, and hightail it out of there. Taking a deep breath, I shine the light onto the body bag and take a look.

It's not Sean. I've never seen this man before, but he bears no resemblance to our missing friend. This person is young and has thick black hair and an impressive mustache. And viewing a dead body isn't as creepy as I thought it would be. With an almost clinical interest, I unzip the bag a bit further.

I realize I have no professional credentials, but it seems to me if this man splattered himself on top of a lifeboat, he should have a pretty messy torso. There should be bones sticking out and lots of blood. He, however, is neatly dressed in khaki slacks and a green striped shirt. The only sign of death is his face, which is way too white and waxen to belong to a living being. This, of course, begs the question—how did he die? It sure doesn't look like he jumped.

How odd. How very, very odd.

Now that my body has stopped quaking from fear, my eyes skim the room and land on the three drawers. As long as I'm here, I suppose I should have a look in them—just to make sure Sean isn't taking the deep sleep in one of them. I pull them open and am relieved to see they are empty. They are cold storage lockers, each equipped with a large moveable tray. My imagination goes into overdrive, and I quickly shut the drawers, zip the dead man back into his bag, and sneak out of the room.

I quickly run to the infirmary, replace the key, and am in the waiting room when a nurse comes in and asks if I need help. I assure her I don't, but she makes me sit down anyway. Twenty minutes later we have determined the alarming flush on my face is due to high blood pressure, and she wants to schedule a visit with the doctor.

While she is looking for her appointment book, I run out of the infirmary and up the stairs as fast as I can—blood pressure be damned!

CHAPTER SIX

"COME ONE, COME ALL. A SHAG LESSON ON THE PLAZA."
According to the daily bulletin, we can learn to shag and enjoy a complimentary glass of what it touts as South Carolina's favorite beverage—Firefly Sweet Tea, a concoction of vodka and tea. Olivia and I know how to shag. She and I are southern girls, born and raised in Bluffton, South Carolina. Olivia lived there all her life until she moved to Wake Forest. When I was six, my parents divorced, and I went to live in Iowa with my mother, but I spent every glorious summer with my father on the May River. I loved his fishing boat and his cozy clapboard house and the lazy summer days spent on the water. Shagging on the beach in the moonlight was part of our young lives, so I'm curious to see how it's taught on a ship in Alaska. Don't know about Firefly Sweet Tea since I've never heard of it, but I'll take their word for it.

The Plaza is three decks high, connected by a series of winding, ornate gold bannisters. We cross the pink, gold, and pale green mosaic tile floor and find chairs near the dance floor. The shag demonstration is already in full swing. The instructor, a cute, dark-haired woman, and her good-looking male partner execute a series of intricate dips and swirls that bear absolutely no resemblance to our shagging of yore.

"Do you think we were doing it wrong?" I whisper to Olivia.

She shakes her head. "This here isn't what I would call authentic. Maybe they learned these steps on the Internet. They're way too fancy for your basic shagging."

When the music stops, the girl claps her hands and tells everyone to get out on the floor. "Come on, y'all. It's really fun. You can do it."

I wonder about the "y'all" because she has a thick accent and I heard her speak to her partner in German, but maybe they shag in Bavaria. I nudge Olivia. "Do you want to join them? At least we know how to do it."

"No, thanks. These people look silly—especially that person in the back waving her arms."

I glance at the waving arms, which are connected to a body that belongs to Melissa. And she is yoo-hooing. "Girls!" She points to a nearby table and smiles broadly.

"That woman pops up everywhere. I don't want to talk to her. Let's go. Make up some excuse. You're good at that." Olivia tugs at my arm, but Melissa and Tina are already at the table and eyeing us expectantly.

"We can't get away right now," I murmur. "Just for a few minutes. Then I'll make up something."

Melissa's blue T-shirt is soaked, and sweat runs down her face. "That was fun. I need to work out more."

"Me, too," Tina echoes. "I just can't seem to lose weight."

Since Tina weighs almost nothing and looks like she could use a double cheeseburger and fries, I smile politely. I have no idea how to respond to that. She also appears not to perspire, which means she either has something wrong with her sweat glands or she is extremely fit.

Melissa stands up and once again yoo-hoos loudly. Her voice rises above the hubbub on the Plaza Deck like a foghorn. "Brittany, Colin! Over here!"

The man is tall—well over six feet—with blonde hair and broad shoulders and an open, appealing face. The woman is blonde and petite, and together they look like an ad for a fitness studio. Honestly, does no one eat anymore?

"Hi. I'm Colin Banning," he says as he extends his hand. "And this is my wife, Brittany. Where are you all from? We're from Texas. I'm a football coach, and Brittany works for the pep squad. She used to be a Dallas Cowboys cheerleader."

"I'm in theater now," Brittany tells us. "The pep squad is a spare time activity"

"That sounds interesting," I say politely. "Do you act? Or are you more behind the scenes?"

Brittany pulls herself up to her full 5'3". "I'm on the stage. I play the ingénue a lot."

Colin wraps his arm around his wife's waist. "Never very big roles, though, sweetie."

Brittany glares at him and changes the subject. "Do you all know how to shag? It looks like an old people's dance."

I stiffen my back and say, "I assure you it isn't. Folks of all ages enjoy shagging."

Brittany snickers. "The way you say it makes it sound like something funky."

I feel the blood rush to my face. "I simply mean shagging is fun, especially when a friend does it with you." Lordy! Stop talking! Olivia makes a zipping motion across her lips indicating the need for silence.

"Brittany and I are celebrating our one year anniversary," Colin says in an attempt to fill the awkward void. "This is our first cruise, and we're loving it. We're looking forward to going ashore at the ports."

I'm listening to him and trying to think where I've seen him before. This man's impressive physique would stand out anywhere. The ship is huge, and there are a few thousand passengers, so it's very possible I've seen him on deck or in a restaurant. No, now I remember.

"I think we saw you in Ketchikan, Colin. You were talking to one of our friends."

He's the man we saw with Sean. The more I look at him, the surer I am.

However, he looks at me blankly. "Don't think so. You must be mistaken."

"No, I'm not. We're concerned about our friend. I've asked all over the ship if anyone has seen him. Maybe he said something to you about staying in Ketchikan?"

I'm obviously being a bit too aggressive because his pleasant demeanor fades. "Told you I didn't see him. Come on, Brittany, we have to go. Hope you find your friend."

Olivia is wiggling her eyebrows at me, which means, "We, too, must split."

"I know I'm right," I say as we head to the elevators. "That's the guy Sean was arguing with."

"You also thought you saw Johnny Depp in the hot tub the other night. Turned out it was a crewmember with a mop. You might need to have your vision checked."

But when my stomach lurches and my heart stops beating, I know there's nothing wrong with my eyes, and I can't believe what I'm seeing. Dirk Harrison, a special friend or—whatever you want to call him— from my trip to Iceland, is walking down the spiral staircase. And he has an attractive, younger woman on his arm.

CHAPTER SEVEN

"What's wrong with you? You've turned the color of paste." Olivia scans my face anxiously. "I told you not to eat those fried oysters last night."

"It's not that," I manage to squeak. "It's someone I see." I point to Dirk and his companion who've stopped to study the paintings hanging in the art gallery.

Seeing him brings back a flood of memories. About eighteen months ago, Olivia and I took a bus tour around Iceland. Fourteen of us walked on glaciers, learned about hidden people and trolls, saw the northern lights, and ate delicious salmon. Dirk was a widower traveling solo on the trip, and he and I…well, we sort of had a one-night stand. I blame it on copious amounts of wine, celibacy since Tony died, and the roaring desire to feel the touch of a man again. Plus, Dirk was extremely sexy. He was much taller than I, which I loved. Dark hair, blue eyes—there was nothing about him I didn't like. Even the fact that one of our group thought he was a murderer—there was an unfortunate death on the trip—didn't dampen my ardor. But the physical distance between us did. He was a lawyer in California, I baked cupcakes in North Carolina. For a while I saw him every month when he came to visit me in Wake Forest, but the better our relationship became, the more I pulled away.

I blame this on my tendency to overthink everything. Things were going so well, it couldn't possibly last. What if we did get together? Would I like his kids? (He had two grown sons.) Would they like me? What if he wanted to live in California? I didn't want to live there.

Even though he must have been confused—considering the enthusiasm for all things physical I displayed when we were together—he kept calling. I would see his name on caller ID and not pick up. Finally, he stopped.

Seeing him now is like a punch in my gut. He has moved on, and the woman with him is gorgeous. Dark, shoulder-length hair, a crisp white shirt with raised collar, tan cropped pants, and fancy sandals with straps wound around her ankles. She looks sensational.

I, on the other hand, do not. The wind on deck has blown my hair into a wild tangle, and my navy polo shirt and denim capris are certainly not fashion-forward apparel. Neither are my comfortable running shoes. I don't run, but they feel good on the feet.

I watch as Dirk and his friend wander through the gallery and sit down at a table at the window. This seems to be a popular place because the chairs are filling up quickly. I notice a poster on an easel and understand why. An art auction is going to begin in twenty minutes.

If you enjoy art, the shipboard gallery is a fun place to visit. Paintings and drawings by various artists are hung on portable screens. Passengers are encouraged to browse and take notes about favorite pieces so they can bid on them at the auction. I have to admit I like some of the colorful work by Peter Max. There are also drawings by Picasso and Salvador Dali lithographs.

"Let's do this," I say to Olivia. "We can sit over there." I indicate chairs behind Dirk so he won't be able to see us. The woman can, but that doesn't matter.

"Why do you want to stay here? I thought we were going to meet Rebecca on the deck."

I forgot about Rebecca. "I'll apologize to her later. Right now we have to spy on Dirk."

A smiling girl offers us complimentary glasses of champagne—designed to relax the potential customers and loosen their wallets.

"Drink up," I tell Olivia, "and whisper when you talk to me." I nod my head at Dirk. "I don't want him to hear."

The auctioneer picks up a mic, and we are ready to begin. He tells us his name is Grant Merino, and he has loved art all his life. He's tall, fairly good-looking, and has a ton of black hair combed straight back and held in place with grease. To be fair, it's probably an expensive pomade, but it looks like bacon fat. He also seems to have boundless enthusiasm.

"This is going to go fast, folks, so don't miss out. What am I bid for this original Peter Max oil painting?" His voice throbs with excitement. "We'll start the bidding at $40,000." His eyes scan the crowd. "I have $40,000. Do I hear $43,000? Going once, going twice—sold for $ 43,000!" He bangs down a gavel, and people begin clapping.

Excuse me? What just happened? I didn't hear anyone bid anything so who in the name of Nancy bought the painting? I turn to Olivia. "Am I nuts? Did you hear anyone bid?"

"Nope. It's the old fire up the group and make them think there are hot items for sale spiel."

"Really? I'm appalled. That has to be illegal. And who would actually believe it?" We stop talking because the art director is holding up another canvas.

"How 'bout it, folks? Are you ready to add something beautiful to your home? Something you will treasure the rest of your life? Look at this beauty by everybody's favorite landscape artist, the painter of light, Thomas Kincade. Who wants to start the bidding?"

Mr. Merino is good. He sells three Kincades in a matter of minutes. His grin and his spiel are infectious, and in spite of my intention to keep my eye on Dirk, I find myself smiling.

Olivia pokes me in the ribs. "You have a goofy look on your face. You don't need a painting, and you certainly can't afford that one."

I glance at Dirk who's in deep discussion with the woman. By now I've convinced myself she's his wife and they're living in a gorgeous ranch in Napa with horses and vineyards. She spends her days overseeing the staff and wandering through their fabulous fruit orchards and flower gardens. Their wine is probably well known in the area. Maybe I can find it at our local Harris Teeter. Are they buying a painting together? Maybe for over the fireplace at their Spanish style hacienda? Although if it's for their hacienda, they probably need something with more vibrant color.

"Here you gals are again! Didn't realize you had an interest in art." Melissa, followed by the ever-present Tina, plops down into a chair across from us.

Good grief! What do we have to do to get away from these ladies! They pop up everywhere we are. Now Melissa raises her hand and bellows, "Hey, darlin'" to the girl serving champagne. "What do we have to do to get a drink?"

I sink down in my chair, praying Dirk is so engrossed in the art, he doesn't hear her. "Don't know much about this stuff myself, but people pay big bucks for it. Say," she changes the subject, "have you seen our friend next door?"

"Do you mean Sean? No, I haven't. Have you?"

She takes a big gulp of champagne. "Nope, but I heard you've been looking for him. He must be around here someplace. If he'd gone overboard, the ship would have stopped to search."

I shudder. "What a horrible thought. And they did stop the ship. Remember when the captain made that announcement? I know we stopped, but not long enough to look for a body. Surely there would have been search lights and more commotion."

"You're probably right. Maybe he stayed in Ketchikan and intends to take a float plane to Juneau and catch up with us there."

Somehow I doubt that very much, but this time I keep my thoughts to myself.

I can't stand up and risk Dirk seeing me, so Olivia and I stay for the entire auction. I'm amazed at how many pieces of art Grant Merino sells. His charismatic personality coupled with his appealing smile makes his patter hard to resist. When he sells an expensive, totally blue canvas to a woman from Ohio and calls it a "wonderful example of color field art," I almost applaud. I wonder how much buyer's remorse these folks will experience tomorrow.

The auction ends, and Dirk and his friend leave— without buying anything, as far as I can tell. I'm ready to go, too, but Grant Merino puts out a hand and says, "Saw you admiring the art. I'll be happy to show you around."

I say, "No, thanks, we have to go," but Olivia says, "I'd love to see more." They both look at me expectantly, so I reluctantly follow them into the gallery.

"Don't you want a special souvenir to remind you of your trip to Alaska?" he says, giving us that mega kilowatt smile.

"I bought a little totem pole. That's plenty for me. We don't have the money for art like this."

He ignores my plea of poverty and jumps right into a sales pitch. "Look at these drawings. Any one of these would make a wonderful remembrance of your cruise." He lowers his voice. "May I speak in confidence? An avid art lover sold us his entire collection, and the only place in the world you can buy one is on this ship." He points to a series of framed drawings. "We are so fortunate."

I peer closely at the drawings. I learned all about them when I was trying to get a master's degree is art history. They are Picasso's doodles—simple drawings of people, animals, or just about anything—using a single, unbroken line. There are wonderful stories about him paying for restaurant meals with doodles he drew on paper tablecloths or napkins. When a manager once asked him to sign a doodle, he declined, saying all he wanted was dinner. He wasn't interested in buying the restaurant.

I always thought Picasso must have laughed to himself when these little doodles sold for a lot of money. People would rave about how he could reduce a complex subject to its basic form with one fluid line. To me they look like scribbles on a piece of paper, but what do I know? Now Grant is telling me I can buy one of these originals for a mere $6,500.

"Look," he says, "Picasso drew this on a napkin. You can still see a bit of color on the upper left edge— possibly made by the great artist wiping his lips after a fabulous coq au vin dinner in a Paris bistro."

This is supposed to be a selling point? There really is no accounting for what people will buy. I turn back to the drawing and notice most of them are signed. "Do you have certificates of authenticity for these? I ask because Picasso wouldn't sign a lot of them."

Grant studies me for a minute without speaking. "I see you are somewhat familiar with Picasso's work. See this one?" He points to a squiggly line drawing of a woman. "He wrote 'pour Jacques' at the top and signed

it Pablo, so he did sign some of them. And we can
certainly authenticate every one."

I don't remember enough about the doodles to discuss
it further, so I thank him and leave Olivia there to look
at the rest of the gallery. When I hear her say, "Here's
one by Leroy Neiman. I wonder if he's any relation to
Neiman Marcus," I know the art director has his hands
full.

CHAPTER EIGHT

I am watching from our veranda as the Golden Eagle glides smoothly through the Gastineau Channel to the dock in Juneau. At first glance, Juneau doesn't look much like a state capital. There are more buildings than in Ketchikan, but the city is surrounded by snowcapped mountains. And since it's accessible only by boat or plane, the dock is a busy place. The Norwegian Pearl is in the berth in front of us, and by-planes take off and land constantly.

I would like to be out on the deck, but I'm afraid I'll meet Dirk if I go out there. I intend to avoid him, and this is a big ship so it shouldn't be that hard to do. Even though I'm the one who never answered his phone calls, it hurts in my heart to know he's found someone else.

Olivia bursts into the room, all giggly because she has just had coffee with Grant Merino. "Isn't he cute? He's nice and tall, and he has a really good body. We went to the gallery and he explained some paintings to me. And look what he gave me."

It's a smudged pencil drawing of a goat. The paper is torn at the edge, and the actual drawing is very faint. "He said he had plenty of them and wanted me to have it." She sticks it in the frame of a mirror on the wall. "I don't particularly like it, but it would be rude to throw it out."

I'm not surprised Olivia finds Grant Merino attractive. She likes men and isn't particularly particular in her choices. Her three husbands were disasters, and the third one put her off committed relationships for good. Ben, the louse, was handsome, athletic, charming, and well-heeled. The perfect husband. His other wife thought so, too, and both she and Olivia were quite upset when they found out old Ben was not only a bigamist, he was also actively searching for wife number three.

I'd warn her to stay away from Merino, but it wouldn't do any good. If I know my friend, she'll hang around with him until she realizes he's a fast-talking, smarmy, creepy con man. This shouldn't take long because Olivia is pretty smart.

"I don't know what this is," I say about the drawing, "but I doubt very much the art director would give you anything very valuable. You didn't buy anything, did you?"

She scowls at me. "Of course not. Although he did say he could give me a really good payment plan."

"I'll bet he did. He reminds me of a snake oil salesman."

Olivia pulls her sweater over her head and tosses it in the closet. "That's because you're upset about seeing Dirk. You're in a bad mood. Aren't we going to get off the ship now? I'm dying to see the Mendenhall Glacier and maybe have a beer at the Red Dog Saloon. Grant says we absolutely have to go there." She puts on a clean top, swipes gloss over her lips, fluffs her hair, and looks at me. "Well, come on. Is that what you're wearing? Never mind. You look fine. No one's going to see you."

I've been in such a turmoil due to seeing Dirk and worrying about the missing Sean that I completely forgot we have tickets for a walking tour around the glacier. It's raining now, and I really don't want to do this, but we each paid $70 for the excursion so there's no turning back. I zip up my windbreaker and pull the hood over my head.

Even in the rain, the Mendenhall Glacier is beautiful. Large chunks of aqua blue ice that have fallen off the glacier float in the lake. I listen to the guide explain how the glacier is continuously retreating and how in forty years it will no longer be visible from the visitor's center.

The guide drones on, and I'm cold. I try clapping my hands together and jogging in place. Others seem to be as uncomfortable as I am. Phoebe and Martin Skofield, the couple we met the night we sailed from Ketchikan, are huddled together trying to keep warm.

"I'd way rather be back on the ship having a nice cup of tea," Phoebe says. "The glacier is pretty, but I've had enough."

I nod. "I'm with you. Guess we can't do much about the weather, though. This is typical for Alaska."

I don't want to chat. I'm freezing, my wet hair is hanging in my face, and my feet are soaked. But Phoebe isn't ready to stop talking. I need to keep my blood moving, so I start down the path around the lake and Phoebe joins me. Our conversation is not very stimulating. I point out a sign that says, "Watch for Bears." Phoebe looks nervous and says maybe we should go back, but I tell her I read if a bear is in the area, so is a ranger. I have no idea how the bear and the ranger coordinate their activities, but they live here and I don't, so who knows. Then our chat turns serious.

"I heard you were asking about that guy in the stateroom next to you," she says. "Were you supposed to hook up with him? He isn't bad looking if you like short men."

Who on earth would have told her that? "We three were simply meeting for a drink. It certainly was no date. How did you even hear about this?"

She looks embarrassed. "Sorry. I don't mean to pry. Our room steward, Sergio, said you had been asking about him. I think I told you Martin likes to be on good terms with the help. Anyway, what I'm trying to tell you is I saw that guy. He was with a very attractive blonde—young and perky."

What! I stop walking. "When was this?"

Phoebe pulls a tissue out of her pocket and wipes her nose. "Darn cold weather makes my nose run constantly. Let's see. When did I see him? It was after we sailed from Ketchikan. Or maybe it was before. I can't exactly remember. He and this girl were sitting in a lounge on the Promenade Deck, and they looked very cozy."

It can't have been after we sailed because that's when I found the ripped Port Pass, but I'm not going to share that with her.

"I don't suppose you'd have any idea who this girl is? See, the thing is, Sean, the guy in the room next to ours, hasn't been seen since Ketchikan. He's a really nice guy, and we're worried something has happened to him, so it would be helpful if you could identify this girl." I say this even though I know she couldn't possibly. There are over two thousand people on this ship.

"Actually, I can. I've seen her with that hunky tall guy. You know, the one that's hard to miss. Big muscles, broad shoulders, really cute. I thought the little blonde was married to him, but I guess not."

Could she possibly be talking about Brittany and Colin Banning, because if so, the little blonde has some explaining to do. But my chat with Brittany will have to wait. We have tickets for a whale-watching excursion after lunch.

Compared to the Golden Eagle, our whale-watching boat is the size of a dingy, and it has also seen better days. The white paint on the Sea Urchin is peeling, and a section of the railing is completely missing. Instead, yellow tape is stretched between metal poles, and a handwritten sign warns passengers to be careful. There are eight seats in the bow, room for perhaps ten people in the stern, and six benches in the main cabin.

As we board the boat, I see Melissa, Tina, the Bannings, the Skofields, and several others run across the pier to the boat. I grab Olivia by the arm and pull her into the cabin and out the door to the other side.

"I don't want to sit with them," I tell her. "Brittany jabbers too much, and Melissa drives me crazy." As I talk, I look over her shoulder. "I think they're going to sit down inside. If we stay out here, we can avoid them."

My friend pulls off her hat and fluffs her hair. "I sure like your people skills. It's a good thing you're mostly in the kitchen at Little Bites."

"That's not because of my people skills," I tell her. "I'm just a better baker than you are."

We don't have time to debate this because the captain begins to talk over the loudspeaker. "Welcome, folks. You're going to see amazing humpback whales today. Down here near the water, you will experience up close all the sounds of these magnificent creatures. One word of caution: I'm sure you all have seen the tape where a railing should be. A whale actually took our rail out when he got a bit too close. Not to worry, it won't happen again, but make sure you stay back from the tape. We don't want any of you to accidentally go swimming."

The boat begins to move and soon we see spouts in the distance. "Every tour boat is required to stay 100 yards from the whales," the captain continues, "but believe me, we will be close enough."

Down here on the water in the presence of these enormous creatures, I feel very small—almost overwhelmed. The captain explains that the loud high-pitched sounds the whales are making are meant to scare their prey. Don't know about their prey, but the noise sure is scaring me.

The boat idles and once again the loudspeaker crackles to life. "Ladies and gentlemen, feast your eyes on Alaska's humpback whales. You are about to be treated to something most tourists never see. They have located food and are beginning a feeding ritual"

It is fascinating. Several whales have formed a circle. Together they dive under their prey and then slowly twist up to the surface, blowing bubbles all the way. The bubbles act as a net and force whatever they've found to the middle of the circle. The whales open their mouths and voila, dinner is served.

As we watch the captain says, "These creatures need a lot of food. One whale needs around a ton a day. Hope you're enjoying this, folks. These whales are mighty entertaining creatures."

"Maybe Tina will switch to whale-watching instead of being a whackadoodle who keeps lemurs in her basement," I whisper to Olivia.

"Hush! That's not nice. Bless her heart, she just enjoys her animals."

When a southern girl says, "bless her heart" she's really saying, "Poor soul. Not much we can do about her." A southern girl is way too polite to tell it like it is. I lived in the North too long, so "bless her heart" isn't in my vocabulary.

Olivia swivels her head. "By the way, where did our friends go? They sure aren't out here watching the show."

I jerk my thumb toward the interior. "They're standing at the counter buying snacks. I've been keeping an eye on them."

A sudden cold wind whips across the deck, and both the water and sky turn an ominous gray. Within minutes we are splattered with fat drops of rain. "I'm not going in," I tell Olivia. "You go ahead, but I'd rather stay here."

The whales obviously don't care about rain. They're still feeding, but I can imagine it takes a long time to ingest a ton of food. It's raining harder, and when I turn and look into the cabin I can't see anything because the windows are so steamed up. Lots of people breathing in there, and I'm the only one out here witnessing this wonderful event.

Or so I thought.

I hear a door open and close but don't pay much attention because the whales are still gyrating in a frenzy, and I'm loving the sight. I feel a movement behind me, and suddenly I'm flailing my arms and legs helplessly in the air right before I hit the water. My first thought is the water's very cold. And the second...well, there is no second because now I'm under the water and the sound from the whales is nearly deafening.

Terrified, I fight to get to the surface. Even though I'm over a hundred yards away from these creatures, the sheer force of their movement as they feed is churning the water. To add to my terror, a whale breaches in front of me. The force of its fluke as it smacks down sends waves over me, and I fear I'm drowning.

Surrounded by these enormous, powerful, awesome mammals, I feel like an ant must feel when a human being walks by on the sidewalk—small, insignificant, and thoroughly frightened. I have to figure out how to get out. I dogpaddle to the side of the boat and begin to scream. The interior windows are still fogged, but maybe someone will hear me.

No one does. And to make matters worse, I hear the engine on the boat come to life, which means the captain has decided to move on. This can't happen. The boat begins to slowly move, and I'm frantic. I yell louder, gulping water with each hysterical scream. My arms and legs are so tired I can hardly move, and I find myself analytically wondering how long I can keep this up before I stop struggling and sink to the bottom. Perhaps I'll land on the back of a whale and he'll ferry me to the shore.

I can scarcely believe it when the cabin door opens and Colin Banning steps out. He pulls a pack of cigarettes out of his pocket and shakes one out— oblivious to the fact that I'm drowning down here. I spit out water and scream louder, and this time he hears me. He rushes to the side and yells, "What are you doing down there?"

Excuse me? I wish I could come up with a snappy answer, but I've got nothing. I flail around a bit until Colin flicks the cigarette into the water, pulls a life preserver off the side of the boat, tosses it to me, and in no time has hauled me onto the deck. He may be short on common sense, but I'm very grateful he's long on brawn.

Once back on the Sea Urchin, someone throws a blanket around me, but I'm still shaking so hard I can feel my teeth rattling. My unplanned dunk in the water is causing a good bit of chatter on the boat. Melissa gives me a sweater she keeps in her tote bag along with a bit of advice.

"Next time you're on a boat, be careful where you stand. I mean, the captain warned us about the tape. What did you do? Lean against it?" She shakes her head. "Not very smart."

Colin really isn't the sharpest knife in the drawer. "So how did you get in there?" he asks almost conversationally. "Did you jump?"

I point to the torn tape where the rail should be. "Seems fairly obvious. I fell." But actually I didn't accidentally lose my balance, fall, or anything else. I am positive somebody pushed me.

CHAPTER NINE

It seems like forever until the little whale-watching boat docks at the pier, we board the Golden Eagle, and I am once again safe in our stateroom. While I dry my hair, Olivia orders a pot of tea from room service. "This is chamomile with some lavender and is good for the nerves," she says. She avoids looking at me as she hands me a cup. "I suppose we should talk about what happened."

"I'm glad you said that," I say as I take a sip. "It was very scary. I didn't lean against the tape. Someone pushed me off the boat."

I watch her face wrinkle into a frown. "I kind of thought you'd say something like that. Please, Julia, use your head. Who on earth would push you off the boat? You're beginning to worry me. Are you getting loony because Dirk is on the ship? Would you like me to get some kind of medication?"

This makes me mad. I mean, my best friend should have my back.

"No, I certainly do not need medication, and I also don't feel like talking to you right now. I can't believe you, Olivia. After all we've been through together, I would think you would know when I'm telling you the truth. Someone pushed me. I have no idea who did it, but I'm absolutely sure it happened."

I'm so angry I storm out of the room and try to slam the door, but it sighs unsatisfactorily to a close. I need to think, and for that I need something sweet. And something with caffeine. The tea tasted like dish water.

I head to a coffee and pastry bar on the Lido Deck and to justify the consumption of more calories I take the stairs.

The rain is gone, and I step into bright sunshine. I follow my nose to a gooey cinnamon bun with white icing and a cup of strong coffee. Normally, this area is crowded with people, but it's 5:00 and folks are thinking about cocktails—not croissants. I select a table in the empty seating area and sit down. I inhale the invigorating fresh air and gaze out at the water, which now sparkles in the late day sun. I've stopped physically shaking, but I'm still shaken by my recent unplanned swim with the whales. I will myself to relax and at least temporarily stop all thoughts of Dirk, Sean, and the dead man in the morgue from swirling in my brain. It's peaceful here, and I'm going to enjoy it.

"Excuse me. Do you mind if I join you?"

I look around at the zillion available tables and chairs and prepare an acerbic reply, but Grant Merino, the art director, smiles charmingly and says, "I know I could sit somewhere else, but I hate eating alone, and I like to talk."

What can I say? I gesture at the chair across from me, and he puts his tray on the table and makes himself comfortable. I notice he has a lovely fresh salad with tomatoes, avocados, and shrimp, and I wonder where he found it because I've never seen it on any menu. We wade through the obligatory pleasantries before we can have a decent conversation. After I assure him it is, indeed, my first trip to Alaska, my room is great, and the food is delicious, I ask him about the art gallery.

"I notice lots of people buy the art. You're good at your job."

He stops eating and looks at me. "Thanks. I guess that's meant as a compliment. I remember seeing you after one of the auctions. You seem to know more about the pieces of art than a large percentage of passengers."

I lick icing off the corner of my mouth. "I almost had a master's in..." I stop because I don't feel like going into that entire story, which will necessitate talking about Tony and the awful shooting.

He's smart enough to know not to press me for an answer. "Are you employed in the art field in—where did you say you lived?"

"I don't think I said, but no, I don't work in a gallery. I just appreciate art. I admire people who can produce amazing paintings and sculptures." I drink the last of my coffee. "I can't draw anything, but I wish I could."

He nods. "Same with me. That's why I love being surrounded by beautiful pieces everyday."

I look at his face, trying to guess if he's kidding. Some of the paintings by well-known artists are good, but there's an awful lot of schlock in there, too.

He finishes his salad and pushes the plate aside. "What do you think of our little gallery? Has anything caught your fancy?"

"I think some of the pieces are very nice, but when you begin the auction by telling folks about the sale you just made of a $40,000 painting, I wonder who you think you're fooling. You and I both know that's just a come-on to get people excited about buying. Don't you worry about authenticity? These people buy in good faith, but I wonder how many are disappointed once the art arrives at their homes." I have no idea why I'm babbling, but he's sitting at my table. I didn't invite him, and he started the conversation.

"It's entirely plausible to think someone paid a high price for a masterpiece," he begins, but I cut him off.

"My ears still work well, and I'm absolutely positive no one bid such an amount. You were simply trying to rev up the crowd. Unfortunately, there were probably several people who actually believed you instantly sold an expensive piece of art."

He laughs. "You've got me. So what's wrong with a little showmanship? It's not against the law."

"No, it's not," I say, "but it would be against the law to attribute a work to an artist and not be able to prove it."

The art director looks like he's beginning to regret sitting down at my table.

"Are you talking about the doodles? I can assure you we make every effort to guarantee the artwork is legitimate. We have very few complaints." His pleasant demeanor and the sun are fading rapidly.

I retrieve the remains of my cinnamon bun and stand up. "I'm happy to hear that. I'll have to come by and take a closer look."

"That would be great," he says. He smiles, but not with his eyes.

Olivia and I are still barely speaking when we head to the Golden Lobster for dinner. It is formal night on the Golden Eagle, and we see all kinds of splendidly attired people on our way to the restaurant. Tuxes, long shimmering dresses, and even some furs. My friend is wearing black satin pants and a sparkly silver top. She has piled her hair on top of her head and skillfully applied all kinds of smoky color around her eyes. I'm wearing a black dress, extremely uncomfortable high heels, and a necklace Tony gave me. I'm pretty pleased with my appearance, though. For once, my hair has behaved and allowed me to style it, and makeup has given my face some much-needed pizzazz. So I'm on a bit of a high as we give our name to the hostess.

Once again, it's hard to believe we are on a cruise ship because the restaurant looks like a typical seafood place on the water in South Carolina. A large sailfish decorates one wood-paneled wall. There is crab netting suspended from the ceiling, and life preservers and framed maps of fishing areas and framed photos of boats.

And there is Dirk and his friend at the table right next to us.

I'm so speechless, I knock over the glass of water the server has just poured. It runs across the red and white tablecloth and soaks the menu. My purse falls to the floor, and I jump to my feet to retrieve it at the same time Dirk leaps to his feet, which results in us banging our heads. I hear the woman gasp and Olivia laugh. I wanted to meet Dirk but not like this. I want to crawl under the table and get away.

Dirk straightens up and rubs his head. For a few minutes, he stares at me, disbelief etched on his face. "This is amazing. I'm very confused, but it's wonderful bumping into you, Julia."

He's trying to make a joke, but I still can't manage to speak. He looks sensational. He isn't wearing a tux, but the dark pants, white shirt, and blazer are smashing. The woman with him is dressed in a simple elegant ivory sheath that I know must have cost a fortune. I don't know much about fashion, but I know that. I feel my face flame as I reach for my purse and stand up.

"I'm still so shocked I don't know what to say except you have no idea how happy I am to see you. How in the world is this possible? I never in a million years imagined I would see you again on this cruise. Or that I would ever see you again." He smiles at me, and I feel my heart melt. I struggle to find words.

"It's nice to see you, too. Are you and your wife enjoying the trip?" I sound stiff and formal, but it's the best I can do. I can't help staring at him because he's way better looking than I remember.

He frowns and then begins to laugh.

"Do you mean her?" he asks, nodding at the gorgeous woman. "She thinks you're my wife, Elizabeth."

The lovely one stands up and extends her hand. "I'm Elizabeth Harrison, his sister."

I realize I've been holding my breath because the air rushes out of my lungs in a whoosh. Now I feel almost giddy. And when I feel giddy, I tend to babble.

"So nice to meet you, Elizabeth," I say, pumping her hand more vigorously than necessary. "This is my friend, Olivia. We live in the country in North Carolina, and we run a little lunch restaurant—quiches, cupcakes, things like that. Actually they're quite good. We're going to try a line of homemade pies when we get home. Noting fancy, just good old downhome cooking."

Olivia shakes her head ever so imperceptibly, and I stop talking.

"I've heard all about you, Julia, or at least I used to." Her voice is soft and pleasant.

I'm trying to think of a response when Dirk saves the day by saying, "Let me see if they'll let us sit together. I think we probably have a lot of catching up to do."

Ten minutes later, we are at a table for four, and Dirk has ordered a very nice bottle of Sancerre, which he must have remembered is my favorite white wine. We order dinner—a nice shrimp scampi for me—but my stomach is so knotted I doubt I'll be able to swallow a bite. While we wait for the food to arrive, Elizabeth tells us she runs a veterinary clinic in San Francisco, loves horses, and has three dogs and a cat named Vichyssoise or Vi for short. Dirk gave her this trip as a birthday present. I sneak a look at her finger and don't see a ring, so I assume she isn't married.

Dirk talks about a lengthy trial he was involved in and about a trip to Hawaii with his sons. I, on the other hand, have moved from babble to silence. The food comes, and as I predicted, the delicious seafood is stuck in my throat. Olivia seems to have no digestive problems and is devouring her blackened salmon. I notice Dirk isn't eating either. As we talk, I feel his eyes on me, which is really disconcerting because the elephant at the table is so huge, it's making conversation between us impossible.

But we go through the motions of civilized behavior, and the dinner finally ends. Elizabeth excuses herself saying she wants to see the show in the theater, and Olivia says she's going to the shops before they close.

Dirk and I sit there, unsure of what to do. When he says, "How about an Irish coffee up at the Starfish Lounge?" I jump to my feet, happy at the chance to be doing something.

We take the elevator to Deck 12 and find a table outside at the bar. For once, the wind isn't blowing at ninety miles an hour across the deck, and the night sky twinkles with thousands of stars. Strategically placed tiki torches throw off just enough light to create a romantic atmosphere. A server brings the Irish coffee, and for a bit we sip in silence. Finally, Dirk says, "So maybe we should talk."

I take a large gulp of the liquor-laced coffee and say, "I'm really sorry. I really don't know what happened." That sounds lame, and I do know what happened. I just don't want to admit it.

Dirk looks out at the water. "I honestly thought we had something there."

"Well, we did. It's just that I thought...listen, Dirk. I stopped taking your calls because everything was perfect, and I knew if we kept seeing each other I'd do something to piss you off or you would find someone younger and prettier, so it was better to end it before I had a broken heart. The distance between us was too much, and what if your kids didn't like me..."

Suddenly all the words, all the dumb thoughts came pouring out. It took the entire Irish coffee for me to purge myself of all my insecurities, and when I finished I had tears in my eyes.

Dirk gets up from his chair, comes around to me, and takes me in his arms. "You really are dumb. How could you ever think those things?"

"I don't know," I mumble. "California is so far away, and I figured you'd get tired of flying across country, and then I felt bad because I don't have enough money to fly often to see you...." He shuts me up by kissing me. I feel my knees sink down to my socks—if I were wearing any—and realize now I should have answered the phone when he called.

One more thing, though. "So you're not seeing anyone?" I whisper.

"Nope. One very silly, attractive, dizzy baker in North Carolina stole my heart. And she still has it."

Well, well, well! Things are, indeed, looking up.

We talk more, and it's probably close to 1:00 in the morning when he kisses me goodnight and tells me we'll spend the whole day together tomorrow. I'm far too awake to consider going to bed, so I go down to the Promenade Deck and step outside. Once the heavy door closes, the music from the Dolphin Lounge fades, and I am alone in the soft night. I stroll slowly to the stern, thinking about meeting Dirk again. This has to be some kind of karma at work. What are the odds that he and I, after so many months apart, would end up on the same cruise ship and at tables next to each other? It almost seems as if fate is trying to tell me something. My mind is a jumble of emotions, and I realize this isn't an optimal time to sort out my thoughts. Instead, I savor the sight of the full moon on the water, and I watch as the wake from the ship builds and disappears.

I'm so immersed in the scene I'm at first confused when a gloved hand is suddenly clamped over my mouth and another strong hand forces me against the rail. However, I don't require a rocket scientist to tell me someone is trying to harm me. A voice, which I can hardly hear over my thudding heart, whispers, "How would you like to swim with the sharks? That's what will happen if you don't stop snooping."

I try to twist to see my tormentor, but the hand holds me firmly in place. Now I'm afraid this person is going to throw me overboard, and there's no one out here to witness it. But out of the corner of my eye, I see a figure practically running toward us. The person holding me shoves me so hard I fall and hit my head on the edge of a deck chair.

I think I blacked out for a minute. When my eyes focus again, I sit up and test my limbs. Nothing appears to be broken, but when I feel my head, my hand touches something sticky.

"My God, Julia! Are you okay? What in the world happened?"

Dirk is crouched beside me, cradling me in his arms. I begin to cry—whether from the shock of being attacked or from pain I don't know—but I'm so happy to see my rescuer I can't speak. He helps me to my feet and makes me sit down. Using the flashlight on his phone, he examines my scalp.

"I don't think you need stitches. It's bleeding a lot, but head wounds do that. Let's get you to your stateroom and get you cleaned up, and then you can tell me what happened."

I'm propped against the pillows on my bed, trying to bat a worried Olivia's hand away from my head. "Please let me put a wet washcloth on it," she says. "It will help the swelling go down. I can't imagine who would do this to you. Or why. We're on a cruise ship, for heaven's sake!"

As Olivia fusses, I notice Dirk isn't saying anything, and I can't read the look on his face. "How did you happen to be out on the deck to save me?" I ask.

"You left your purse in the lounge. When you weren't in your room, I figured you'd gone for a walk. Olivia told me you liked to do that, but let's leave that subject for a minute." He gets to his feet and paces around the room. "I'm familiar with your work, Julia. You have an uncanny ability to get yourself in a mess of trouble—albeit through the best of intentions. You've obviously stumbled into something on this boat, and we need to figure out what it is before something serious happens."

I toss the washcloth to the floor and stand up. The world spins for a minute, and I grab the edge of the table for support. "I think this all has something to do with Sean's disappearance. I know something evil has happened to him. I just have to figure out what." I start to wobble to the door. "And I'm going to find him."

Dirk puts his arm around my waist and leads me back to bed. "Who is Sean? And what are you talking about? And not tonight. I don't know what's going on, but wait until tomorrow, and let me help you. I want to make sure you stay safe."

Hearing him say this makes me feel extremely good. "Okay. If you insist." I give in easily because if I take one more step, I'll fall on my face.

CHAPTER TEN

It's still dark when I wake up the next morning. Olivia is snoring peacefully with the sleep mask over her eyes as I stumble into the bathroom and take a look at myself in the mirror. Not a pretty sight. There's a painful lump on the side of my head and black circles under my eyes. I look like I've been in a fight.

I pull on some clothes, intending to get coffee at the breakfast buffet. As I gingerly comb my hair, my eyes fall on Sean's torn Port Pass. I try to ignore it, but it's calling to me like the Lorelei luring sailors to their death on the rocks. I don't want to be lured to my death, but I sure would like another look at Sean's room. Maybe I missed something important.

I tuck it in my pocket and silently creep out of the room. The hall is empty. There isn't even a room steward in sight at this hour. I tiptoe to Sean's room and insert the Port Pass in the lock and open the door. Something instantly feels wrong. I can't put my finger on it, but the stateroom looks different. The steward was probably here to clean, but it's something else. For instance, the windbreaker I saw hanging over the chair is now lying across the bed. And the photo that was on the table is now face down on the floor. I can't imagine a steward would leave it there. Did Sean do this? Is he really on the ship and shacked up with some woman? He wouldn't throw the picture on the floor, though, would he?

Judging from the hair standing up on the back of my neck I would say someone—not an employee—has been in here. I pick the photo up and am about to put it back on the table when a thought occurs to me. Maybe Sean wrote something on the back of the picture—like dates or the special occasion.

I gently open the clips and pull off the backing. I turn the photo over, and there is, indeed, writing on the back. Courtney, Lisa, and Lily. San Francisco 2016. Of course! Now I recognize Fisherman's Wharf in the background. Now that I know their names, their smiling faces tug harder at my heart. I have to find out what happened to their daddy and husband.

A piece of paper falls out of the frame and flutters to the ground. I scoop it up, intending to stick it back in the frame with the photo—after I look at it. I am truly shocked at what I see. The paper is the size of a driver's license and seems to be some kind of ID card—for the FBI. Just to make sure I'm not having some kind of myopic distortion event, I read it again, but it still says Sean Mauer, Federal Bureau of Investigation.

All kinds of questions race through my mind. Sean obviously hid this in the frame. But why? Did he know he might be in some kind of danger and wanted to hide his identity? Was he on this cruise because he was doing a job for the FBI? Was the photo on the floor because someone else searching the room threw it there? It occurs to me that if someone did search the room, and if that person knows where Sean is, said person must also realize his cell phone is missing. That idea gives me chills. Also, how did this person get into the room? Sean is missing, and I have his Port Pass.

I put the photo carefully back in the frame and place it on the floor, just in case the unknown person comes in for another look. I stick his ID card in my pocket and leave the room.

I need more coffee and access to my laptop because now that I have names, I intend to Google Sean. The breakfast buffet is crowded, and I wait in line at the coffee bar. When it's my turn I fill a to-go cup with coffee, cream, and sugar, grab two sweet rolls from a tray, and head to my room.

Olivia is still sleeping, and I don't want to disturb her, so I grab my laptop and head to the Sun Deck. There will be folks exercising up there, but they'll be concentrating on fitness and not me. I walk along the deck until I'm alone and sink down into a chair.

Fortunately, the Wi-Fi works all over the ship. I figure since Sean works for the FBI he probably lives in the vicinity of government buildings. I bring up Google and type in Sean Mauer Washington, DC. Nothing. Next I try Maryland. I have a friend who works for an agency in Washington and lives in Maryland. Still nothing. Maybe Virginia. Zero. I lean back in my chair and try to think. There are FBI offices all over the country. What if Sean travels for his job? He wouldn't have to actually live in Washington. He also probably wouldn't live in Idaho or Kansas, but somewhere relatively close—like maybe Pennsylvania.

Two Sean Mauers come up. One is seventy-five years old and the other fifty-one—and I almost whoop with joy when I see the fifty-one-year-old has a Courtney associated with him. Bingo! I think I've found Sean and his family.

Excited, I run his name through 411.com and find his address. 3710 N. Bryant Street, Greensburg, Pennsylvania. I click on street view and see a sturdy brick house that rises at least three stories. Large pots of red geraniums sit on the concrete stoops on either side of the front door. I swing around to the back of the house and see a vegetable garden, a gym set, and an above ground swimming pool. These images must have been taken in the summer because a riot of blooming sunflowers, poppies, zinnias, and snapdragons surrounds the back of the house. On this day, the sun was shining, and this wonderfully colorful picture of a happy home is tearing at my soul—which makes absolutely no sense since I hardly know this man. I realize it will be difficult to explain to Dirk, but sometimes you meet someone and have an instant connection. You chat for a few hours and feel like you've known each other forever. That's sort of how I feel about Sean. As I've said before, I felt he's a genuinely nice guy.

Out of curiosity, I Google his wife to see if I can find any additional information and can't believe my luck when I instantly find a Courtney Mauer who owns an art gallery in Greensburg, Pennsylvania. I open the web page for White Swan Fine Arts and see a well-done, colorful display of available work at the gallery. The current exhibition is a series of paintings by the local artist, Leon North. They are faintly reminiscent of canvasses by Edward Hopper. Leon North uses blocks of colors without much shading or nuances—the people and buildings are simply and starkly there. He allows the power of the images to speak for themselves, and I have to admit I like them.

I click on 'About the Gallery' and read about Sean's wife. She's a Pittsburgh native, graduate of Penn State, and owner of the gallery since 2011. There is also a picture of her with a golden retriever and a little black-and-white curly-haired dog. In a personal remark, she says, "I've loved painting and any kind of creative activity since I was a little girl. Opening this gallery and being surrounded by beautiful things is a dream come true."

I know I shouldn't be doing this, but I'm not going to listen to the voice of reason in my head. I'm going to email Courtney Mauer. I'm not going to say anything like, "Hey, just wanted to let you know your husband is missing." I'm going to be very subtle, and maybe if she and I can eventually have a conversation, I'll be able to learn something that will help Sean. I open my laptop and bring up her website, click on 'Contact' and write the following message:

Hi,

I've been looking at your website and have fallen in love with all the work of Leon North. I'd love to buy a print of The Café. The image of the woman sitting by herself holding a cup of coffee has haunted me since I first saw it. Could you please tell me how to go about purchasing it?

P.S. Love your golden. I have one, too.
Best Regards,
Julia Greene

I don't have a golden, but I thought a personal touch would be good. The act of writing the email has made me feel more in control. Now I have to put some makeup on my bruised face and go meet Dirk.

Satisfied with the morning's investigating, I close my laptop and look up and see Brittany Banning rounding the corner of the jogging track. Her blonde ponytail is bouncing and her lime green shorts and pink halter top are attracting male followers. Three men, two of them visibly out of shape, stagger behind her. She and I need to have a little talk.

I need to talk to her. As she approaches, I step out onto the track and hold up my hand like a traffic cop. "May I have a word with you?"

She stops but doesn't look happy. "Can't it wait? I'm trying to do laps."

"Not really. I need to talk to you now."

"Then start running." She takes off down the track. When she turns around and says, "Are you coming?" I have no choice. I tuck my laptop under my arm and run after her.

Running is not my thing. My knees are stiff, and I'm out of breath before I've gone thirty steps. Still I manage to say, "I understand you went out with Sean Mauer" before I begin to wheeze.

"Who?"

"Please don't make me say that again," I gasp. I manage to say, "Couldn't we please find somewhere to talk?" before I sink to my knees on the ground.

She steps over me and says, "I have four more laps to run. After that we can talk."

Thank heavens! I lurch over to a chair at the coffee bar, sit down, and try to catch my breath. Maybe I'm just a bit out of shape. It wouldn't hurt to get a bit more exercise. I order a caramel latte with whipped cream and vow to start running tomorrow.

By the time Brittany joins me, I've had two caramel lattes and am feeling quite refreshed. She sits down and orders a bottle of water.

"So what do you want?"

"I need to talk to you about Sean Mauer."

"Who?" She delicately blots her face with a napkin and smiles at a man at the next table.

"Sean Mauer. Someone saw you talking to him."

"So?"

Lordy! This is like talking to a goldfish. "He hasn't been seen for a while, and I just wondered if you could possibly know where he might be."

"Why all the questions? Do you have a thing for him?"

"Of course not! I'm simply worried about him."

"Get to the point. What do you want?"

She looks like she's about to bolt, so I decide to throw a Hail Mary. "He hasn't been seen since we left Ketchikan, and you're the last known person to have talked to him. If something has happened to him, the authorities would probably be interested in that info. See where I'm going here?"

Maybe blondes really aren't very smart because she jumps to her feet and says, "I surely wasn't the last..." then catches herself before she says more. But it doesn't matter because I have all I need. She is, indeed, the woman seen having a tête-à-tête with Sean. But why? Is she romantically involved with him? I can't believe that, so it has to be something else.

CHAPTER ELEVEN

Dirk is already seated in the Sail Away Grill. I don't need breakfast since I've already consumed two sweet rolls and two lattes, but I'm craving something savory—and it isn't polite to allow someone to eat alone, so I fill my plate with scrambled eggs and bacon. For a minute, I stand at the buffet and study him. He looks wonderful. This morning he's wearing a blue polo shirt and khaki pants. For the zillionth time, I wonder if we could possibly have a future together. Even though he's a lawyer in Sacramento and I'm a quiche baker in North Carolina, maybe distance won't matter.

We have a whole lot to learn about each other. Several years ago his wife died of cancer. He must have had a wonderful marriage—just as I did—because he hasn't found anyone to take her place. His two boys are grown. One is about to become a doctor, and the other is studying law. But that's about all I know about him. The times we were together were spent...well...not talking about serious things.

Dirk looks up, sees me, and flashes that gorgeous smile. "So what's up, buttercup? You look wide awake and ready to go. How's your head?"

I've almost forgotten about that. I feel the bump and say, "It's okay. I've had a busy morning."

He raises his eyebrows and stops eating. "What have you been doing? I thought we agreed to do the investigating together."

"I didn't exactly investigate."

"What does that mean? I can tell you're up to something. How about starting at the beginning?"

So I tell him about meeting Sean, and my gut feeling about him, and his disappearance and finding the torn Port Pass and searching Sean's room and finding his home address on Google. "That's about it," I say. "There's also this." I pull the FBI card out of my pocket and hand it to him.

As I talk, I watch all kinds of emotions cross his face—disbelief, amusement, anger. He takes Sean's ID card from my hand, and his mouth tightens as he reads it. "What have you gotten yourself into, Julia?" he says in a low voice. "You say you found this in a picture frame?"

I nod. "Do you think he's on a case here? Why else would he hide it?"

He reaches over, takes both of my hands, and looks at me intently. "I sincerely wish you would stop breaking into rooms and doing all this investigating. You're going to get hurt, and that's going to make me very upset. Now that we've found each other again, I don't want anything to happen to you. I think maybe it's time to inform the ship's captain about your friend's disappearance. Let the authorities figure this out."

"No!" I shake my head vigorously. "If we do that, I would have to tell them about finding Sean's torn Port Pass. And admit I searched his room." I feel my face turn red. "I don't want to do that." When he doesn't reply, I plunge on. "You don't think I'm crazy, do you? I know there's something bad going on here."

"In this case I don't think you're entirely crazy. I'll have to admit it's strange to find this guy's FBI card in the back of a photo. My only concern right now, though, is your safety."

This makes me feel great, but it doesn't dampen my enthusiasm for sleuthing. "I think this has something to do with the ship stopping that night we sailed from Ketchikan. According to our dining room steward, ships never stop, but ours did. Didn't you notice it, too? And then the captain made that strange announcement."

"We were at dinner in the Steak House. We did seem to slow down, but I guess I wasn't paying that much attention. And you're right about the announcement. The captain was hard to understand."

"I know something happened that night," I say. "And I know something has happened to Sean. You have to believe me, Dirk, Sean is a really nice guy. The fact that he hasn't come back to his room, and no one's looking for him or even misses him puzzles me."

Dirk finishes the last of his waffles and sits back in his chair. "Are you sure he isn't shacked up somewhere with a passenger? Just let me say there are a lot of willing women on this ship."

I want to ask how he knows that, but I swallow the words. Instead I say, "He simply doesn't seem like that kind of man. And if he wanted to be on the prowl on this ship, why would he have a framed photo of his family in his room? Seems to me that would be a major turnoff to any lady coming for a nighttime visit."

"This is probably true, but let's not worry about him right now. Come to the art gallery with me. I saw something there that I might actually like to buy, and I want to have another look."

I'm disappointed he doesn't want to do any investigating, but I go with him to the Promenade Deck. I stop at a table full of Alaskan articles for sale and convince myself I need a small blue purse with a long strap that will be perfect for shore excursions.

At this time of day, there are only a few passengers looking at the artwork. Dirk and I stop in front of three paintings of a woman—at least I think it's a woman. The colors are vivid, and I like the bright reds, oranges, and violets, but the ugly distortion of the face disturbs me. And her head is way too small for her corpulent body.

"Are you seriously thinking about buying one of these?" I ask. I peer at the name on the label beside the paintings. "I'm not familiar with this artist."

Dirk grins. "I'm disappointed you don't like these. I was going to buy one for you."

"That sure isn't necessary. Where do you plan to hang something like this in your house? It's a good thing you're not married."

"That's pretty cold, Julia—especially since these aren't the ones that interest me. I like that one," he says, pointing to a large canvas of a ship in stormy seas. "It reminds me a little of George Bellows's paintings. And not nearly as expensive. It would be a nice reminder of a wonderful trip."

That makes my heart beat happily. I'm glad he thinks this is a wonderful trip, and he also never ceases to amaze me because most people associate Bellows with his Ashcan school paintings of New York City. They don't know he spent time in Maine and painted wonderful seascapes. But Dirk does.

"I have no idea if this would be considered a good painting. I just like it," he says. "I know this is your bailiwick. Is it any good?"

"If you like it, it's good. That's all that matters. And for what it's worth, I actually think it's well done, but my opinion doesn't count."

He puts his arm around my waist and pulls me close. "It matters to me. It's great to have an expert confirm my good taste. I think I'd like to buy this before it comes up for auction."

"I'll go find the art director," I tell him. "He knows me, so maybe he'll give you a better price."

I trot off to the little office at the end of the gallery. The room is cluttered with framed paintings stacked against the wall, art books, and pamphlets advertising the gallery. Even the small wooden desk is covered with folders of papers and brochures. I don't see Grant, the enthusiastic art peddler, anywhere.

I notice a sign on the door that says, "Back at 3:00 for the art auction." To make sure the painting Dirk wants isn't sold, I decide to leave a note for the art director and look around for a piece of paper. I don't want to touch anything on his desk, but there's crumpled paper in the wastebasket. I can use that. I retrieve what looks like a brochure and smooth it out. It's not a brochure, though. It seems to be one of Picasso's doodles. This can't be right. Who on earth would throw away a Picasso—even a doodle?

I sit down in the chair and study the drawing. It's of a bird, and the line, which is supposed to be unbroken, seems tentative—as if the person drawing was being cautious. Picasso didn't draw that way. His lines were smooth and strong.

Puzzled, I search through the wastebasket for more. There's one other. I don't get it. Who throws out a Picasso? Maybe an art student was trying to learn Picasso's technique by copying his work. I remember when I studied painting we copied old masters. One professor was particularly interested in chiaroscuro, so we spent hours trying to copy the shading in Rembrandt's masterpieces—unsuccessfully, I should add. Could this be the same thing?

Another, more sinister idea crosses my mind, and I try to push it away. I remember reading an article about art forgery on cruise ships and how prevalent it is. I look at the doodle I'm holding in my hand. If I hadn't found this crumpled up in a wastebasket but saw it framed in a gallery, would I believe it was authentic? Of course I would.

Clutching the drawing, I run out to the gallery to look at the framed doodles. Dirk smiles as I come toward him, but I don't have time to chitchat. Instead, I grab his arm and pull him along.

"I have the wildest hunch, and I have to show you something. Surely I can't be right." I pick up a pen and a piece of paper from a table. The paper is meant for passengers who want to jot down notes for the auction, but right now I have another use for it.

"You see this?" I try to draw a straight line in the shape of a bird. "See how the line looks uncertain, and it doesn't resemble a bird. I mean, I can draw adequately, but this doesn't look anything like a Picasso. I didn't draw with confidence, and neither did the person who drew this. There's definitely a wobble."

Dirk peers closely at my drawing and the discarded one I'm holding in my hand. "Okay. If you say so. I'm no good at this, Julia, but I'll take your word for it."

I stop in front of a framed Picasso doodle of a horse and study it closely. The one unbroken line should be sure and confident. Is it?

"Does this line look confident to you? I think I'm detecting a wobble."

Dirk seems amused. "I think I'm detecting a wobble, too. What are you trying to say?"

"Please don't think I'm crazy, but I believe this might not be a real Picasso." I quickly move to the next one. "This isn't either. They're all drawn by the same hand, and I think they're all fake."

He looks skeptical but so far hasn't told me I need serious medication. Another thought occurs to me. If these are fake, could there be others, too? My eyes scan the art hanging in the gallery. There are Dalí lithographs with hefty price tags. Ditto paintings by

Max Ernest and Peter Max. I simply don't know enough about these artists, and I realize I need to learn. But first I have to do something. I pull out my phone and snap ten pictures of the drawings. Then I search my contacts looking for a number.

One of the professors, Lescano Ceballo, in the art department at Columbia remains a good friend of mine. He was my mentor when I studied there, and he and his wife often invited me to their apartment in the city for dinner. I remember now his specialty was Picasso. I shoot him an email asking if he would be willing to look at some pictures, and when he instantly agrees, I send him ten of the doodle photos. My only comment is "What do you think of these?"

I turn to Dirk and ask, "Would you be terribly upset if I ran away for a bit? I want to do some research on my laptop."

"Would it do any good if I objected?" Dirk smiles, though, so I figure he isn't all that upset. Just promise me you're not going to run around getting into trouble."

This annoys me just a tiny bit because I'm not used to anyone telling me what to do, but I smile and nod. No point in getting into an argument now. I wave goodbye to Dirk and take the glass elevator to Deck 11. As I float above the Promenade Deck, I see Dirk looking up at me. He doesn't look happy, so I blow him a kiss. He still doesn't look happy.

CHAPTER TWELVE

As I step out of the elevator, I nearly bump into Melissa and Tina, who are walking with their heads down, deep in conversation. Melissa looks up and gives me a toothy smile.

"Good morning. You're out and about early."

"Just having a bit of exercise." I pat my stomach, which is full of eggs, pancakes, and sweet rolls. "It's good to begin the day with a jog."

Melissa eyes me skeptically. "You don't look like you were running. You have crumbs on your shirt."

I brush them off. "Must have blown on me up there on the track. It's windy this morning."

She throws a look at her sister and says, "Tina and I were wondering if you'd like to join us for a special treat."

What to say, what to say? I can't say I'm busy because she didn't tell me when, and I can't say I'm not interested because I don't know what it is. I fold my arms across my stomach and give what I hope is a thoughtful gaze. "Well, that depends..." I begin.

"I can promise you it'll be real interesting." She lowers her voice even though there's no one around to hear us. "Did you know there's a verified medium onboard? And she's agreed to hold a reading for a select group of people. It's going to be tonight in her cabin."

I want to ask her how you verify a medium, but I wisely keep my mouth shut.

"You can bring your friend, too. What do you think?"

I have to admit I'm fascinated, but I've never been to a medium. I tell myself it's because all that stuff is hokum, but the truth is I'm afraid of what I might hear. I don't need to know my destiny.

"What time is this? Olivia and I are quite busy, so we probably won't be able to come."

Melissa puts her arm around my shoulder—a totally unnecessary gesture. "I'm not taking no for an answer. It's fun and there will be others there. The medium's name is Madam L'Oeil, and she's quite perceptive."

"L'Oeil? Doesn't that mean *eye* in French?"

Melissa claps her hands in delight. "That's so clever of you, Julia. It is, indeed, a French word. She chose it because she can see into your soul. You don't have to pronounce it correctly. Just say Oy."

"Lordy! Okay. How did you meet Madam L'Oeil? I haven't seen her services advertised in the daily paper."

"I overheard her reading another passenger and introduced myself. I have some psychic ability but not enough to work professionally, and I thought she might be able to give me some tips. Anyway, it's at 10:00 tonight in cabin E685 on Deck 5. See you then."

The elevator door opens, and the ladies step in. Melissa wiggles her fingers at me. "Ta ta until tonight. Don't be late."

The door closes, and I hightail it to my stateroom. Olivia is lying on her back in bed with the sleep mask still in place. I pull it up and peer at her.

"I know you're awake. Get up. We have things to do—and we're invited to a reading with a medium tonight."

She scowls at me. "First of all, I need some coffee and then perhaps some eggs benedict and then a period of relaxation for digestive purposes. And I don't like mediums—or should that be media?"

"I think it's mediums, but right now that doesn't matter." I open my laptop and begin my Google search. "I found something interesting in the art gallery, and I have to check it out."

For the next twenty minutes, I'm fascinated by what I've found. Art forgery is apparently a big problem on cruise ships. Passengers are often duped because they don't know enough about what they're buying, and they have no way to research a possible purchase because Wi-Fi is sporadic on the open seas. They end up paying insane prices for what they believe to be authentic pieces. First the champagne loosens them up, and then the shill bidders planted in the audience fire them up. Limited editions by famous artists like Chagall, Renoir, and Dalí are bestsellers but are also the most copied. One passenger paid an enormous price for a Dalí only to discover it was a forgery when he got home. Now I'm convinced the Picasso doodles are forgeries. But what do I do about it, and how do I prove it?

This leads me to think about Sean, so I bring up the FBI site. I see the Bureau investigates a lot of different crimes—such as civil rights violations, violent crimes, and terrorism, but I don't see anything about art forgery. I Google "Does FBI investigate art forgery?" and learn it does, indeed. There are several articles about agents going after big-time forgers. Maybe the Picasso doodles wouldn't qualify as major art, but maybe they are only the tip of the iceberg.

The snake oil salesman has to be involved in this.

And then there's this.

Dear Ms. Greene,

We are delighted to hear you're interested in purchasing a print of 'The Café.' We love Leon North, our local artist, and are proud and happy others enjoy his work. We would be delighted to send the print to

you via FedEx. The signed print is $383, which includes shipping. We accept all major credit cards and we ship immediately. Your print will arrive in two days. Let us know what you would like to do.
Warmly,
Courtney Mauer

I shoot off a reply. I can't have the print delivered in two days because I won't be home. I also don't have $383 to spend on artwork, but I'm going to ignore that fact for now.

Hi Courtney,
I definitely want the print and I'm so excited to think about having it in my home. I was an art major in college and have always loved the work of Edward Hopper. Mr. North's paintings remind me of him. Please don't send the print yet. I'm on the Golden Eagle on a cruise to Alaska and won't be back in North Carolina for a while. Lovely cool weather here.
Best regards,
Julia Greene

There. That should do it. I know she hasn't heard from her husband, so she has to be worried. I only hope she takes the bait.

I've convinced Olivia to come back to the gallery with me by promising to sit with her while she eats eggs Benedict. It will be my third breakfast, but you've gotta do what you've gotta do. I'll run it off when I start my jogging program.

The crowd at the breakfast buffet has thinned. Folks are getting ready for their shore excursion in Skagway. Olivia orders her eggs with a side of blueberry waffles and settles into a chair at the window. My stomach feels like I've swallowed a watermelon, but I put two warm cinnamon rolls on my plate—just to keep her company. As we eat, I try to tell her what I've discovered at the art gallery, but she's too busy consulting a map of Skagway to listen.

"It looks like we'll have some fine shopping opportunities," she says, pointing a perfectly manicured green nail at a picture of a building. "We can go to the Red Onion for lunch and still have plenty of time to hit all the shops."

Oh, goody! More food—and I'm frustrated that Olivia can't seem to think about anything but shopping. I'm even more frustrated when Melissa saunters up and sits down.

"Still eating, Julia?"

This is uncalled for, but since I want her to go away, I smile sweetly and ignore her question. "Olivia and I have been planning our day in Skagway."

Melissa doesn't appear to have heard me. She leans her face close to mine and says, "You're a strange person, Julia. I can't figure you out. My sister was just saying we don't know much about you."

I feel my heart beat faster, which is either a sign of high blood pressure or an impending temper outburst. There is always one busybody on every trip who feels the need to go beyond pleasant, innocuous chatting, and Melissa seems to be ours.

"Why would you want to figure me out? We're passengers on a cruise ship. Once we dock in Seattle, we'll never see each other again." I look to Olivia for help, but she's busy sopping up egg yolk with a piece of toast.

"Well, forgive me for trying to be friendly. And forgive me for being interested in people. I like to know what makes my friends tick. For instance, I overheard you say you studied art in college. I'd love to chat with you about French Impressionism. Just the other day I said to Tina I wished I had a knowledgeable friend."

Say what? Did I say that?

"When did I say that?"

"I think it was that day at the auction. We chatted quite a bit about paintings and techniques."

We did? I remember being preoccupied because Dirk was there, but I'm pretty sure I never mentioned my art background because I'd already decided the art director was a snake oil salesman, and I certainly wouldn't have offered any information about myself.

I appeal to Olivia. "Did I say I studied art?"

She pauses, coffee cup in midair. "As I recall you mumbled a lot of stuff. You might have mentioned your college experience. I do remember you weren't making much sense."

Melissa looks at Olivia with interest. "Really? Why wasn't she making much sense? I did notice she seemed distracted."

Enough of this nonsense. I stand up and say, "Come on, Olivia. We're late."

"We are?" she asks. "What are we late for?"

"That thing. Have you forgotten? Nice seeing you again, Melissa. Have a pleasant day."

Olivia is still clutching her napkin as I pull her away. "Honestly, that woman annoys me so much. She pops up everywhere we are. It's as if we can't avoid her."

"She's not that bad," Olivia says as she tosses the napkin on a table. "You just don't like to make small talk. Sometimes I'm really surprised at your lack of people skills."

To my dismay I watch Melissa walk toward the art gallery. I'm hoping she's going to the lounge next to it, but she greets Grant Merino at the entrance and the two of them go into the gallery and disappear among the rows of paintings.

"Well, darn it!," I say to Olivia, "I want to talk to Grant, but not with Melissa."

"I don't want to talk to anyone. Why don't we enjoy the lovely scenery outside?" Olivia says.

"Not right now," I tell her. Now Melissa is leaving the gallery and is heading to the shops. This is my chance. There are people sitting in the lounge across from the gallery. They're laughing and drinking Bloody Marys and are paying no attention to me. Just to make sure I'm invisible, I walk past twice, but no one looks my way. Good. What I have to say to the art director should have no witnesses.

I slip into the gallery and head straight to the office. To my surprise, the art director isn't here. I must have missed him, and right now I'm so nervous about being caught snooping, I forget about Grant and get busy. I have no idea what I'm looking for. Since we're probably dealing with forgeries, I don't expect anything as obvious as invoices, but there has to be something.

But there isn't. The art director isn't an orderly person and apparently has no private life because there's no personal correspondence, but if you're engaged in forgery, maybe it's best to be colorless. The only drawer in the desk is stuffed with bills, a menu from a Juneau restaurant, and several notes from someone named Ashley, who's in the sixth grade and likes the "picture of the lady with the crown," which I assume means the Lady Liberty's Head painting by Peter Max.

The wastebasket has been emptied, and there are no crumpled doodles lying around. There are, however, three framed Dalí prints against the wall behind his desk. I examine them closely, wondering if they could possibly be fakes. The signatures at the bottom of the prints appear exactly alike, which is almost impossible to do if an actual human is writing. And they look like they could have been made with a stamp. I say this because the ink is not consistently dark. I pull out my phone and snap a few pictures to send to Lescano Ceballo. Aside from the few pieces stacked against the wall, there's no other work, and I wonder where he keeps the rest of the canvasses. The auction always features new art, so it has to be stored somewhere. There are also no records of sales in the gallery, nor can I even find an order form. So if there are no records here, where are they? In his cabin? Does he share his cabin with another crewmember? I'm thinking no because technically he isn't part of the crew. And where is his cabin? I have no idea, but I think I know someone who might.

Olivia.

CHAPTER THIRTEEN

"This has to be the dumbest thing I've ever heard of. How exactly do you propose to do it?" Olivia is in one of the shops looking at jewelry. She's holding a ring we would have to sell our business to afford.

"He likes women," I say, "and you know him. You could get him to ask you to his room, and then you could have a quick look around."

"May I just say hell to the no! I'm not getting anywhere near the man."

I knew this would happen! It hasn't taken long for Olivia to get tired of the snake oil salesman. "I thought you liked him," I say. "Don't I remember you saying something about his great body?"

"He's smarmy. I'm not getting anywhere near him. Why don't you fix yourself up and go after him? You know—eyelash extensions, more makeup, maybe a push-up bra."

She must be crazy. "I'm not doing that!"

"Well, I'm not either. It's that or nothing."

The salesperson overhears our conversation and gently removes the ring from Olivia's hand.

"There has to be a better way," I tell her. "I have to try to prove the doodles are fake."

The woman behind the counter is now eyeing us sharply, so I wiggle my eyes in the direction of the deck and walk out of the shop. Olivia follows me, and for a few minutes we stroll in silence past the tables of clothes and gifts displayed on the deck. Finally, she says, "If I can tell you his cabin number, would that help? Maybe you can figure out a way to get in."

Surprised, I stop walking. "Do you actually know that?"

Her face turns a bright red. "Don't judge me. I had drinks with him and after a few Moscow Mules he asked me to go to his room. Being the pious person I am, I demurred and told him I'd come to his room after I freshened up. I wanted to make sure my makeup was still perfect, and I needed to recharge my cell phone—just in case I had to call for help. He gave me his room number." She sees my face and says, "Don't worry. I certainly didn't go, and I have no idea if he waited for me because I've avoided him since then. He will chase anything that speaks to him and he's...oily. That's the only word I can think of. So you're on your own. His room is on Deck 8, Cabin E104. Right now, he's probably on the Sport Deck at a little table in the corner. He needs several cups of coffee in the morning to, as he calls it, 'rev his engine.'" She shudders. "I can't imagine anyone actually believing his cheesy line. And he smells of garlic. So you have fun. I'm going to the spa to get my nails done."

I watch her walk away and tell myself to get up and go see if Grant is getting his caffeine fix, but the sun is shining and a pair of whales—full of morning vigor—are cavorting in the sparkling water. I watch until one of them slaps the water with its fluke and dives under. Playtime is over. The scenery is mesmerizing, and I seem unable to stand up, until I see Melissa and her sister coming across the deck in my direction. Fear of being trapped in an agonizing conversation with the ladies propels me to my feet, and I scoot up the staircase before they can see me.

I make my way around folks in bathing suits and lounge chairs by the pool, inhaling the strong aroma of coconut sun lotion as I walk past. A tired-looking woman shepherds two little girls who are punching each other into the kiddie pool and then sinks into a chair and waves to a man serving mimosas. I can't say I blame her. The father is probably still sleeping.

I climb up the stairs to the Sport Deck. There sure are a lot of energetic sweaty people up at this hour of the morning. They're running, walking, and doing painful-looking pushups. I spot Grant at a table next to the pizza station. The plate in front of him has two slices of pizza and a cinnamon roll. A balanced breakfast. I notice the pizza only has one bite out of it, which means he'll be there for a while. Good. I jump in the elevator and push the button for Deck 8.

As I glide down, I wonder how I'm going to get into Grant's cabin. Since I don't possess super powers, staring at the door and wishing for it to open isn't going to work. Maybe I should have given this scheme a bit more thought.

The only folks I see on Deck 8 are cabin stewards making up rooms, which gives me an idea. I lurk in the hall until I see a steward push his cart to room 104 and open the door. I figure it takes about fifteen minutes to clean a room so I walk down the length of the hall, cross by the elevators, and walk down the other side. I make this circuit three times, then peer into Grant's room. The bed is made, but I can see wet towels on the bathroom floor. Another march around Deck 8 and back to room 104. This time I watch the steward walk into the cabin with clean towels and place them on the towel rack.

As he prepares to leave the room, I make my move. I put on my best smile and say, "Oh, good! The door's open. Silly me. I left something here last night and was afraid I wouldn't be able to get it today. I would ask Grant, but he's terribly busy."

The man nods, but it's obvious he doesn't understand much of what I'm saying. It's also obvious I'm not the first female to request access.

However, my intention to enter the room is clear. I glance at his nametag. "Grazie molto, Luigi. I promise I'll close the door when I leave." I beam at him, hoping I look like a normal person and not someone intent on snooping.

He shrugs, which I take to be the equivalent of "none of my business," and steps aside. Bada bing, bada boom, I'm now in the room! I wait until I see the service elevator door close with him in it, then get to work.

I must say, for a man who lives on a ship for months at a time, his room is extremely impersonal. There aren't any photos of family members or books or even magazines. The bed is neatly made, and there's no prescription medicine in the bathroom. The closet holds the normal amount of clothes, but nothing exciting.

This search is yielding a big fat zero. Grant must keep all his records on his laptop, which makes sense. And his laptop is with him. I saw it on the table next to the pizza. I'm ready to leave, but just to make sure I've looked everywhere, I pat the pocket of a raincoat hanging in the back of the closet. When I feel something, I stick my hand in and pull out a small notebook. I flip through the pages and see it appears to be full of names, addresses, and phone numbers, and it must be fairly old because these days people keep all this stuff on their phones. Still, I want to have a closer look, so I tuck it into my pocket and sneak out of the cabin.

An hour later, Olivia and I are getting ready to watch our ship dock in Skagway. I've inspected the little address book I found in Grant's cabin, and while it was entertaining to see how he rated the different ladies he dated—a 10+ for someone named Charity, to a 1 for Molly—it didn't contain useful info. However, there was one interesting notation. There's an address in Skagway, and he had drawn a small bird next to a phone number. It probably means nothing, but since Picasso drew birds as part of his doodles, maybe it does.

CHAPTER FOURTEEN

I love Skagway the minute I step off the ship. As Olivia, Elizabeth, Dirk, and I walk down Broadway, my imagination takes me back to how it must have been during the exciting gold rush days. For thousands of men and women—drunk with dreams of massive wealth—this was the jumping off point to the Yukon and the gold fields. All they had to do was get their horses, equipment, and themselves safely up and over the White Pass. Many never made it. Those who did came back to Skagway and spent their precious gold on nights of booze and women, both of which were in abundant supply.

I am fascinated by the meticulously restored buildings, and it's easy to imagine raucous, alcohol-fueled miners spilling out of bars and shooting each other in the street. The Red Onion Saloon on the corner of 2nd and Broadway was one of the most famous and extremely busy bordellos in Skagway. It is now a busy restaurant, and the servers dress like the glittering ladies of the olden days.

Farther down Broadway, I spot the gold dome of the Golden North Hotel gleaming in the sunlight against the backdrop of the snowcapped Coast Mountains. Today it's home to several shops, but it was a thriving establishment during the gold rush. According to my guidebook, it also has a ghost. A prospector promised a woman named Mary he would come back for her after he found his fortune. He never did, and Mary still haunts the place waiting for him.

I'm dying to explore this fascinating place, but before I do, we are going up a mountain to a musher's camp. Let me say right here I love dogs and have looked forward to this excursion since we boarded the ship. My secret bucket list wish is to participate in the Iditarod driving a team of magnificent huskies—only in my dreams the dogs resemble my own puppies—a slightly overweight springer spaniel and a black-and-white elderly mutt.

We gather at the waiting area for our transportation, and I'm surprised to see Melissa, Brittany, and Phoebe. "Are you all having a girl's day?" I ask. "Where are your husbands?"

Phoebe adjusts her fanny pack around her waist. "Mine hates dogs. Actually, he hates all animals. This wouldn't be a fun trip for him."

I look at Brittany. "Mine is busy," she says. "And it's surely none of your business."

Fair enough. I guess it isn't.

"And Tina wanted to go to a Scrabble tournament," Melissa offers. "I think it's just a shame she doesn't want to see all these sights."

We climb aboard the unimog, which is a tank-like vehicle designed to conquer all terrains and won't tip over on steep ascents. Dirk and Elizabeth sit next to each other, and Olivia and a man she met on the ship are together in the front. Brittany and Phoebe have managed to avoid Melissa and have seats in the back. I sit at a window and try my very best to ignore the fact Melissa is barreling down the aisle in my direction. I close my eyes and pretend I'm sleeping, but it's no use because I feel her sit down beside me and jab her elbow into my side.

"This is great?" she says. "We'll have a nice chance to chat. You don't fool me, Julia. I know you're awake."

I open my eyes slightly. "Sorry. I'm terribly tired. Thought I'd nap a bit."

"Nonsense. This will give us a chance to get to know each other."

I give up. I'm going to have to talk, so I turn around and look at Melissa. She's dressed in full safari gear—khaki pants, a khaki shirt, and wide-brimmed khaki hat. Her glasses hang on a chain around her neck. She opens a bag and pulls out a can of bug repellent.

"Mind if I spray this? I need to protect myself."

"I don't know where you think you're going, but I can assure you it's not the Amazon jungle. And I do mind if you spray that stuff. You can't do that in a closed vehicle, and I think others would object, too."

She puts it away and zips the bag. I hope maybe she's sulking because she isn't speaking, but no such luck. After a few minutes of lovely silence, she says, "So what's your story, Julia? Are you married? I suppose not since you're always with that man."

I can't put into words how much this annoys me. Melissa is a passenger on a cruise. I'll never see her again. She certainly doesn't need to know my "story."

"Melissa, please forgive me, but I don't like to talk about my private life." I'm trying not to be rude, but I don't want to share personal details with her, and I certainly don't want to discuss Tony.

"Okay, then I'll tell you about me. I'm not married. Never have been. I've always been more interested in a career. Tina and I live on a farm outside Akron, Ohio. We have chickens, goats, a swan, three dogs, and a huge vegetable garden. I love the country life."

Melissa's fingernails indicate otherwise. They are long, perfectly shaped, and painted a bright red. They don't look like nails that deal with chicken, dog, and other types of poop. I point this out, and she says, "For heaven's sake, Julia. I wear gloves. Okay? What a dumb remark. Anyway, Tina was married once. Her husband left her, though, and she's never recovered." She looks at me earnestly. "You have no idea how devastating it can be to lose your husband, even if it is through divorce. A loss is a loss."

I want to tell her a divorce and death aren't the same—the divorced spouse is still walking around drinking mojitos and enjoying life, while the dead one, well, isn't—but I don't want to chat with Melissa anymore, and we stop talking because the vehicle is rocking and bouncing up the nearly vertical ascent.

"No need to worry, folks," Nick, our guide, calls from his seat in the front. "These unimogs are made to do this."

Nevertheless, I'm relieved when we reach the top of the mountain in one piece, and I can get out.

here are barking dogs everywhere—magnificent animals with thick fur and hard muscles. "They're eager to get going," Nick yells over the din. "Find a sled and get in."

The "sled" has wheels and seats for six people. Ten strong, excited Alaskan huskies are harnessed two by two to each sled. Melissa, Brittany, Phoebe, Elizabeth, Dirk, and I get in and find seats. This time I'm next to Phoebe. Brittany and Melissa are in front of us. A musher standing in the back yells "Mush!" and away we go.

The speed almost takes my breath away. We are really moving. I can feel the dogs' power as they effortlessly pull our sled along the trail and deep into the Tongass National Rainforest. The musher has no reins. He yells "gee" and "haw" when he wants the dogs to go right or left. It's very impressive, and I wonder how you teach a dog to do that. My dogs practice selective understanding so we would probably end up in Kentucky if I tried voice commands.

When the ride ends, we are permitted to pat and talk to the dogs. As I rub a head with gray and black fur and astonishing blue eyes, I'm amazed at how physically strong he is yet so gentle with me. Melissa is standing next to me so I say, "Give him a pat. He's a very nice animal."

"That's okay. I believe you."

"No, really. Feel how strong is body is."

"Thanks, but no. I'm allergic."

Huh? "Don't you have dogs?"

"I do, but I'm allergic to huskies. There's a certain dander in their fur."

"Really? I did not know that. Will you be able to play with the puppies?" We are walking toward the area that holds the newest arrivals to the camp. I pick up a very young puppy, and it immediately nuzzles into my neck. Reluctantly, I offer it to Melissa, but she backs away.

"No thanks. It might pee on me. I don't want to ruin my outfit. And I think it's time to go." She points to the others gathered around our guide.

This time I've planned ahead., Dirk, Elizabeth, Olivia and I head to the back of the unimog and sit on a bench. There's no room for anyone else. Brittany and Phoebe are in front of us. As we bounce down the road, we're quiet. I'm content to sit and relive the marvelous dog sled experience. I don't realize I'm staring at Brittany until I notice something isn't right. I nudge Dirk and whisper, "Do you think her hair is askew?"

"What?" he says too loudly.

"Her hair. It's crooked. The ponytail should be in the center of the back but it's off to the right."

As if she hears us, Brittany reaches up, gives her hair a tweak and the ponytail is back where it belongs.

The unimog lets us off at the waiting area and we walk the short distance to Broad Street. Fortunately, Olivia,

Dirk, Elizabeth, and I are the only ones who opt to stay in Skagway. The others intend to return to the ship. I'm starving, but I really want to see the town before it's time to go. We can eat later. I'm all for exploring now.

"We have to go in some of these buildings," I say to my friends. "There's so much exciting history here."

"You two go ahead," Dirk says. "I'm going to buy an ulu knife." He points to a display of the knives, which are basically large blades with handles, in a store window. "I've always wanted one of these. They're good for skinning animals. And you can use one to cut blocks of snow to build an igloo."

"Do you do much igloo building and animal skinning in California?" Olivia asks.

"Very funny. The truth is, I think it will look great on my desk. It's an intimidating piece of cutlery and obviously isn't used to peel grapes."

Olivia pulls out her map. "I'd like to browse in the gift shop across the street. Do you want to come, too, Elizabeth? How about you, Julia?"

I do not. I didn't come to Alaska to waste time shopping. "You guys go ahead. Let's meet in front of the Red Onion Saloon in half an hour."

Once alone, I pull Grant's address book out of my pocket and consult the page with the bird drawing. According to my map, I'm not far from it. Ahead of me I see a house with what appears to be people hanging out of a second story window. They aren't fighting because there's no noise. In fact, there's no movement at all. Intrigued, I walk faster until I'm standing under the window and am amazed to see this is the address I'm looking for. And these aren't real people hanging out of the window. They are actually well-painted wooden dummies. The female figure is dressed in a red satin dress with a low-cut bodice. Gold ringlets cascade around her face, which has a bright red mouth, sultry brown eyes, and pink cheeks. She's leaning with one arm on the sill. A male figure stands next to her with an arm draped over her shoulder. He's dressed in a dark suit and top hat and has a handlebar mustache. As I stare at them, a loudspeaker suddenly blares, "Come on in! Don't be shy. You know you want to."

Startled, I jump back and prepare to sprint down the road, but the front door opens, and a smiling woman with astonishing orange hair coiled on top of her head steps outside. She's wearing a lavender satin floor-length gown with a lace insert that barely conceals a pair of cantaloupe-sized breasts.

"Come in, dearie. You're welcome to look around."

Dearie? Who talks like that?

"I didn't mean to disturb you," I say and try to back away, but the woman walks toward me and extends her hand.

"I'm sorry. They tell us to say that. They think it makes the whole thing more authentic. I have no idea if people said 'dearie' in the olden days, but there we are. A paycheck is a paycheck. I'm Belle." She winks at me. "I'm the madam here."

"Thanks, but I have to be going." I pretend to check my watch. "Yes. I really must..."

"Nonsense. Come on in. You'll love it, and it's all fixed up exactly as it was in the gold rush days. This house is an exact replica of an old time bordello." She smiles. "It's all pretend, of course. No hanky panky going on here."

I must admit, I'm curious. It isn't often you're invited to a brothel—even a make-believe one. Belle moves aside to allow me to enter. "Feel free to look around. There are some interesting bedrooms upstairs. Please excuse me now while I help the other guests."

I don't see anyone else, but maybe they're all visiting the bedrooms. I tell myself I'll make a quick tour of the house—so I'll have something fun to talk about at dinner—and then leave to meet the others.

I wander into the first room and read the placard above the door. I'm in the parlor. The room is done in bordello red. Red tassels dangle from red velvet lampshades. A very uncomfortable-looking red velvet couch is against a wall. Every available surface is covered with knickknacks: figurines of women with parasols and ball gowns and nude figures of women reclining on chaise lounges. Heavy velvet drapes block out most of the sun. The room feels claustrophobic, and I get out quickly.

The sign above the door of the next room says "Music." A life-size dummy of a woman with blond hair and dressed in a flowing, green silk gown sits at a player piano. On the walls are black-and-white photos of miners trekking up the mountain to the Yukon and celebrating their gold strikes in Skagway.

I jump in alarm as the piano suddenly begins to play. A door opens at the end of the room, and another female dummy, this time wearing a gaudy purple dress, glides toward me on some kind of mechanical platform. The figure holds a tray with glasses filled with a liquid.

"I am Rosie, your hostess. Please enjoy some sparkling Gold Miner Liquid Gold," a recorded voice says as the figure stops in front of me.

Even though I know this is intended to entertain tourists, I'm slightly scared. It all seems a bit creepy. I try to move away, but the figure moves with me.

"Please take a glass," it intones.

"No, thanks. Nope. Nein. Danke. I really don't want one."

"Please take a glass."

Obviously, this mechanical pest isn't programmed to understand a response and has no intention of taking no for an answer, so I pick up a glass from the tray. It is surprisingly cold and bubbly, as if it has just been poured. This seems to satisfy Rosie because she glides away. I look around for a place to ditch the glass and, seeing none, carry it with me as I climb the stairs to the second floor. The steps are narrow and carpeted, and as I mount them I wonder where the other people are. There's no sound coming from above me.

The first bedroom I enter has a large collection of dolls on a double bed. It seems strange to see dolls in a brothel until I read a sign on the bedside table. The bedroom belonged to Annabelle, the daughter of Miss Charlotte. I wonder who Miss Charlotte was and why she brought her daughter to live here.

I peek into the next bedroom. Male and female mannequins wearing old-fashioned underwear are entwined on a bed. Since I have no way of knowing if they are as animated as Rosie downstairs, I quickly back out. I'm quite familiar with the bedroom activities of consenting adults, so I don't need to watch a tutorial.

In the hall, I see a sign that says, "Cookie's Chamber" and an arrow pointing up. Up means climbing sagging, steep steps that end in a narrow hall. There are two rooms. The first is obviously a maid's room. There's a twin bed with an iron headboard and a quilt covering a thin mattress. A black-and-white maid's uniform hangs over the back of a chair and a blue-and-white chamber pot is next to the bed.

The next room has no furniture, but the sign above the door says "Cookie's Chamber." I step in, wondering why Cookie had to live way up here. Was Cookie a person? Or the family pet? The room is smaller than my closet at home. From end to end, it measures four big steps. There is a small window, but it's high up on the wall. I nearly trip over a rolled-up blanket in the corner. When I stretch out my arms, I can almost touch the walls on either side.

I've seen enough. I don't know what this room would have been used for in a brothel, but I have no desire to find out. Time to leave.

A sudden sound behind me makes me twirl around in time to see a retreating figure and the door slam shut. I also hear the unmistakable sound of a key turning in the lock. More annoyed than alarmed, I call out, "Unlock the door, please. This has been interesting, but I have to go now."

When there is no answer, I pound on the door and jiggle the knob. "Hey, do you hear me? People are waiting for me. Fun is fun, but I have to go." Still nothing. I hold my breath and listen intently for a sound, but there's nothing but silence. This is ridiculous. I look around for something to bang against the door, but save for the rolled-up blanket, this room is empty. Even the small window is too high to reach.

I'm being a real dummy. I will simply pull out my cell phone, call Olivia, and ask her to come and rescue me. However, a message on my phone says, "No Service." This isn't good. I wave it around, thinking the action might miraculously bring it back to life, but no such luck.

To make matters worse, a voice, barely above a whisper, comes through the vent in the ceiling. "You shouldn't have snooped. Too bad you're so nosy. No one can hear you, and they will all leave without you."

Now I can't breathe—and I have a pain in my chest. Terrified that I've used up all the oxygen in the room and am in imminent danger of dying, I sink down to the floor. If I had any doubt before about nefarious doings, I sure don't now. I have to figure out a way to get out of here. And to do that I have to fight down the panic that's threatening to overwhelm me. I force myself to take deep breaths and sing something. The only song I can think of is 'God Bless America.' That should work, but to sing it I have to stand up. After a few weak bars, I feel silly and give up.

Panic is still there—bubbling in my throat. The ship sails at 7:00. According to my watch, it's 3:47. Olivia, and hopefully Dirk, must be wondering where I am. Would they look for me, or would they think I've gone back to the ship? Surely Olivia knows I'd wait for them. She'd try to call me, and what would she and Dirk think when I don't answer my phone? Dirk will know something's wrong. *He'll find me*, I tell myself. My heart sinks. No, he won't. He has no idea where I am. And the ship won't wait. It will sail away without me.

I sit back down on the floor and concentrate on breathing deeply, which doesn't seem to be working well. My breath is ragged and coming in gasps. I tell myself someone will come soon to unlock the door, but I can't make myself believe it.

The next time I glance at the window there's no more bright sunlight—just the glow that comes in late afternoon. Maybe more folks will come to the house for evening entertainment. Hopefully, they'll come upstairs. In case people have already arrived, I get to my feet and stomp on the floor as hard as I can. When this produces nothing, I do my best version of River Dance until my legs give out. I go back to pounding.

It has to be late now, but I'm afraid to look at my watch. My fists hurt from the relentless assault on the door. This seems hopeless. The ship will sail away without me, and there's no scheduled stop between here and Seattle. My passport and most of my money are locked in the safe in our room. Will Olivia take them with her? I check my phone again. Now it needs to be charged, and there's still no service.

I go back to stomping and yelling. I'm so busy making enough racket to be heard in Ketchikan that I don't realize the door is open and Belle is standing in the entrance with her hands on her hips and a scowl on her face.

When I see her, I throw my arms around her and say, "Hallelujah! You've saved me! I'm free! How can I ever thank you?"

Belle peels me off her and says, "You can thank me by getting out of here. How did you get locked in? I found the key on the floor in the hall. And why are you even up here? This is off limits to tourists. Your pounding scared the guests downstairs. Some are convinced the house is haunted."

I'm so relieved, I hardly hear her. "Do you have any water? I think I'm severely dehydrated," I say.

"Did you hear me? How did you get up here? The steps are always blocked off to the public."

Puzzled, I say, "I followed the little sign that said Cookie's Chamber. There was even an arrow pointing upstairs."

She looks at me as if I'm crazy. "There's no such sign. What in the world are you talking about?"

"There's a little placard above the door. This is your house, so you should know that."

"There certainly isn't. If you don't believe me, have a look for yourself."

Even though I'm extremely eager to get away, I step out of the room and look up. There's no sign. But I'm sure there was. I'd like to argue the point with her, but there's no time. I brush past her and race down the stairs. "I'm sorry, but I can't talk now," I yell. "And I'm sorry for the noise." I want to add she needs to search her house because someone deliberately locked me in and whispered through the air vent, but I have to get to the pier before the ship sails. I can worry about who wants to harm me later.

As soon as I reach the street, I start to run. I pull out my cell phone, forgetting it needs to be recharged. I'm chugging past the Red Onion Saloon when a voice calls out, "Julia! Wait a minute."

I don't have time to wait, so I wave to the unseen voice and keep running. The next thing I know Melissa is next to me, and she isn't even out of breath. How is this possible? I'm gasping like a beached flounder, and she sounds like she could recite the Gettysburg Address.

"I saw your friend, Dirk, and he said he was concerned about your whereabouts."

"Late for the ship," I croak. "Must get to the boat."

She grabs my arm. "Slow down. Look." She points to her watch. "It's only 5:48. The ship sails at 7:00, and we're only fifteen minutes from the pier. Here, drink this." She presses a bottle of water into my hand. "You look awful."

I slow to a walk and gratefully take a big gulp. "I'm really glad to see you," I say between swallows. "Someone locked me in a house back there."

Melissa looks shocked. "Who would do something like that? Do you think the person was trying to rob you?"

"No. It probably has something to do with..." Me and my big mouth. If I weren't so shaken from being held captive in a strange house, I'd have been more discreet with my words. But Melissa seems genuinely concerned, so I say, "I've been so worried about the guy in the cabin between us. He's disappeared, but I know he's still on the ship. Maybe someone doesn't want me to hunt for him—although I have to admit that makes no sense. And then there's the dead guy on top of the lifeboat. How did he die? I need someone to explain how a body can fall from a great height and remain intact. Crazy things are happening."

"You poor thing. I can see how upset you are. Have you reported your concerns to the ship's authorities?"

I shake my head. "I haven't yet. I keep hoping Sean Mauer will come back. I know I'm probably making a big thing out of nothing. I'll feel like a fool when he turns up with some lady on his arm. And as far as the dead guy is concerned?" I shrug. "That I truly don't understand."

I finish the water and feel better. I really am grateful Melissa is still in Skagway.

"Say," I say, "weren't you going back to the ship after the musher camp visit?"

She nods. "I did go back. But I got to thinking about French fries at the Red Onion. They're supposed to be fabulous, so I came back to get some." By way of proof she shows me an empty takeout box.

By now we've arrived at the dock, and I'm greeted by an agitated Dirk waiting at the gangway. "Thank heavens, Julia! I've called and called, but you aren't answering your phone. Olivia is on the ship because she thought you might have already boarded. Why didn't you tell us where you were going? We've been worried sick."

I realize I have a death grip on Melissa's arm. I wasn't even aware I was holding on to it. "It's a long story. I'll tell you later. Right now I want to get on the ship and go to my cabin."

"I'll walk her to her room," Melissa offers. "It's right next to ours."

"Nice of you," Dirk replies gruffly, "but I'll take over from here." And with that, he peels me off Melissa and walks me to my door.

CHAPTER FIFTEEN

It's 10:00 and I'm ready to fall asleep.

"I don't understand why we're doing this if you're so tired," Olivia says. "We wouldn't be missed if we skipped this...whatever it is."

She and I are in the elevator on our way to Deck 5. As the doors open at each floor, we catch a glimpse of nightlife on the Golden Eagle. There's a particularly lively party happening in a lounge on the Promenade Deck. Three laughing women bounce into the elevator, realize we're going down, and jump off.

"We're going because Melissa was nice to me today when I was feeling frazzled. You know what, Olivia? I think I've misjudged her. She was genuinely concerned about me. So she talks a lot. And she's a bit nosy. Well, she's a lot nosy, but that's not a crime. I might actually start listening to what she says. Too bad her sister is such a zero, but maybe I've misjudged her, too."

Olivia arches her eyebrows at me. "You're babbling a bit now. Everything okay?"

"I'm not babbling, I'm trying to stay awake. If I close my mouth, my eyes will close. I can hear my bed calling. It's saying, 'Julia, where are you?'"

Olivia is still rolling her eyes when the elevator stops at Deck 5. This deck has a distinctly different feeling. There are no people chatting, laughing, or milling about. The corridor is empty as we search for the room.

"Are we above water level?" Olivia asks. "I've never been down this far."

"I haven't either. The morgue doesn't count. It feels like a dungeon down here. The fortune-telling business must not pay very well."

We stop in front of the door of an inside cabin next to the laundry room, and I have to admit I'm having second thoughts. Bed sounds a whole lot better than participating in some kind of spooky séance. As I stand there debating a flight to the upper regions, the door opens and I peer in. It's dark except for flickering candle light. I turn around and bang into Olivia. "That's it for me. I'm out of here."

But it's too late. Suddenly the door opens wide, and a woman wearing a cream-colored off-the-shoulder blouse, wide olive-green belt, an ankle-length turquoise, red, and cream skirt, and stiletto-heeled high boots glides toward us. The full skirt swishes as she walks. On her head is an elaborate pink, green, and purple turban, and around her neck are multiple necklaces made of colored stones. I stare in admiration at her long false eyelashes and marvel she can hold her eyes open—eyes that are rimmed in thick black liner.

"Come on in. You must be Melissa's friends. Sorry about the no light situation. Had to turn them out because I was checking for negative aura. It glows in the dark. I'm Madam L'Oeil. Take a seat."

I wonder where. Phoebe and Martin Skofield are sitting on a small couch, and Melissa is perched on the edge of the bed. Another couple I've never met shares the only chair. Melissa pats the side of the bed, indicating we should join her. I don't want to. I want to leave, but Olivia sits down.

I feel I have to be polite so I say, "So where's your sister? Isn't this something she would enjoy?"

"She is, unfortunately, ill. I wouldn't recommend eating sushi at the outdoor cafe on the sundeck. I'm afraid she didn't listen to me when I warned her about the combination of hot sun and raw fish."

"Sorry to hear that," I murmur.

In the center of the room is a small round table with a cloth-covered object in the middle. The windowless room feels claustrophobic, and there are too many people in here. I remain standing. I lean down and whisper in Olivia's ear, "I'm worried about using up all the oxygen. I already feel lightheaded."

Olivia pretends she can't hear me, and the rest of the people are making small talk. I look around for something to do and spot some brochures on the table. Just the thing. I'll read one.

Madam L'Oeil

Madam L'Oeil, world famous medium, was born in Amiens, France, on the cusp of Cancer and Leo, to which she attributes her extraordinary psychic gifts. She can remember the smallest details and is passionate about her ability.

L'Oeil means eye *in French, and Madam L'Oeil uses her inner eye to see deep into your soul. She has tremendous insight into all things ethereal and paranormal and is able to advise you about marriage, sex problems, finances, job, crimes, children, and UFO encounters.*

Madam L'Oeil can put you in touch with loved ones who have crossed over.

Madam L'Oeil is also available for phone consultations.

If you are in need of an exorcism, please contact Madam L'Oeil. She knows someone who can perform one.

Wow! This Madam L'Oeil seems to be quite a woman. I still want to leave.

Finally, the medium claps her hands and asks for silence. "You have come here to receive messages from the other side. I can't promise who will step forward to speak. Please close your eyes and clear your mind of all transient thoughts and focus on your loved ones."

With that, she sits down at the table, folds her arms across her chest, and closes her eyes. I take this opportunity to study the woman. She is wearing a lot of makeup that appears to have been spackled on so it's difficult to guess her age, and due to the poor lighting most of her face is in shadows. However, I notice tiny rivulets of sweat are already gleaming on her forehead. Her eyebrows are pencil thin, arched black lines, and the hair peeking out from the turban is black—too black to be natural. I can't put my finger on her accent. It's a cross between southern and something European. It's not foreign, but it's not American either. It's an accent someone conjures up when she's trying to fool people.

After a few minutes of silence during which we all squirm uncomfortably, Madam L'Oeil reaches for the cloth covering the object on the table and sweeps it away. I almost laugh. I'd imagined a crystal ball or a Ouija board or something connected with the supernatural, but it's a snow globe. A simple snow globe. Inside the globe is the naked figure of a woman sitting under a tree and circling the base of the globe is a tape with the words Madam L'Oeil in gold paint.

Madam L'Oeil raises the globe high above her head, shakes it, and gold glitter cascades to the bottom. "This is Irina," Madam L'Oeil intones. "She is my spiritual guide and will tell us when spirits enter the room."

"I think I saw that snow globe in the gift shop at the Seattle airport," Olivia whispers. "She sounds batshit crazy."

The Skofields are whispering, too, but the medium is undeterred. "Irina, we are waiting. Do we have a guest?" Irina must have answered in the positive because Madam L'Oeil closes her eyes and presses the palm of her hand to her forehead. "I have a woman stepping forward. She has black hair. Who has lost a loved one with black hair?"

"Are you kidding?" the man in the chair yells. "That could be anyone."

Madam L'Oeil scrunches her eyes tighter shut. "She's wearing an apron. Kind of heavy. She is speaking. I think she's foreign."

Phoebe Skofield gasps. "Tell her to go away. I don't want to talk to her."

Madam L'Oeil opens her eyes and looks at Phoebe. "I can't tell her to go away, sugar. The spirits come and go as they please. Do you know this person?"

"Yes. No. I don't know. I want to leave now. Martin, come on. Let's go."

"That could be my grandmother," Melissa says. "She's deceased, and she was from Poland."

Madam L'Oeil shakes her head. "This is a somewhat older woman. I would say maybe in her late fifties. She's telling me to ask about Sarah. And she's limping. Maybe an accident to the leg?" Madam L'Oeil scans the room. "Anyone know who Sarah is?" She stares pointedly at Phoebe.

"I had a dog named Sarah," the woman in the chair offers. "She ran away, and we never found her."

"This person says it's not a dog. She's cradling her arms. I think it's a baby."

Phoebe turns a ghastly white and sinks down in the couch.

"That's enough," Martin Skofield yells. "I don't know what you're up to, lady, but you're upsetting my wife with this crap."

Phoebe looks terrible, and Madam L'Oeil is wringing her hands. "Please don't be upset. I've asked the lady to leave. Believe me, it's not my intention to cause trouble." She forces a smile. "Let's go on, shall we? There are more spirits waiting to speak."

"I've had enough," Olivia says in my ear. "Do you think we can get out of here now?"

I'm all for that. I'm about to stand up when Madam L'Oeil says, "A man is stepping forward. He's tall, has dark hair, and is very handsome. He also has a hole in his chest—right about at heart level."

"What kind of a hole?" the woman in the chair asks. "Does it go all the way through his body?"

Martin interrupts. "Kind of a ghoulish question, isn't it?"

"I'm just curious," she replies. "Like, is it a big hole? Can you see through his body? That would be cool."

"I don't see an exit point," the medium says. "To me it looks like a bullet hole. This man must have been murdered. Shot right through the heart."

I know she's speaking more, but there is suddenly such a roaring in my ears, I can't hear her. And I am frozen to the floor. I try to make myself run out of the room, but my body doesn't seem to work. I don't believe in any of this nonsense, but could she possibly be talking to my sweet, dead Tony? Is he really in the room? Next to me Olivia is still as a statue, so I know she's thinking the same thing.

"Does anyone know this person? He's fairly insistent about talking to someone here." Madam L'Oeil looks at each one of us intently. "Come on, people. One of you must know him."

I cannot speak. I will not speak. I don't believe in mediums. And if it is my Tony, our conversation should be private, not in front of these folks. But it can't be my Tony—can it? Olivia reaches over and puts a comforting hand on my arm.

The medium has her eyes closed again and is rocking back and forth. "This man says he loves someone in this room very much and is sorry he had to leave the world so soon.

He mentions a place called Franklin Street. Does that mean anything to anyone?"

I know I'm not breathing. This can't be happening. Franklin Street is in Chapel Hill, North Carolina, where

Tony and I met. Every student at UNC knows Franklin Street. We used to meet at Spanky's for lunch. Who would know that? Is it Tony?

"He says, 'Tell her to stay in her lane.' What on earth does that mean? Does anyone have an idea?"

"I think it means to mind your own business," Melissa offers. "I've heard them say that on TV."

"Thank you. Very interesting. Anyone else want to say something?"

"I'd like to say this is getting boring," Martin says. "No one seems to know this guy, so maybe we need to move on."

Sweat starts to pour down Madam L'Oeil's forehead. "I want a spirit to connect with someone. I can't understand why this isn't working."

The woman in the chair yawns. "Is the guy still here? He must be getting bored, too."

"Very funny," Madam L'Oeil mutters. She waves her hand in the air. "Okay. Be gone. He left. And that's all for our session today. There are no more spirits waiting."

"Why aren't there? What did you do with them? I thought you couldn't send the spirits away," the unknown woman yells. "This is all fake. I want my money back. I had some things to say to someone."

"We're supposed to pay for this?" Olivia whispers. "I don't think so."

Madam L'Oeil retrieves the cloth and covers the snow globe. "That's it. Irina says no more. Y'all can go now."

Y'all? That's not very French, but I'm too upset to worry about it. I allow Olivia to take my arm and lead me out of the room. As we pass the medium, Olivia says, "Bonne chance, Madam. That's good luck in French. I have a feeling you're going to need it."

I don't realize I'm shaking until I try to hurry down the hall to our cabin. Melissa is behind us, and I don't feel like talking to her, so I'm trying to walk fast. However, my legs feel like pudding, and I'm afraid I'm going to fall down. Olivia takes a firmer grip on my elbow. "Keep walking. We're almost there."

Apparently, Melissa doesn't feel like talking either because she is silent, and when we reach our room, and I turn around to say goodnight, she is nowhere to be seen.

CHAPTER SIXTEEN

It's 3:12 a.m. and I haven't closed my eyes. I think it has to do with the very disturbing thought that Tony may actually have been trying to talk to me, and I wouldn't listen. I tell myself over and over I don't believe in this stuff, and the medium is as phony as they come, but what if she's not, and she is genuinely able to contact people who have died. Common sense and logic tell me she can't, but my heart is wishfully thinking maybe she can and did, and I missed a chance to talk to Tony.

There's no point in tossing and turning. I get up, pull on a sweatshirt over my pajama top, and stick my feet into slippers. Careful not to wake Olivia, which is a useless worry since I could bang cymbals right next to her head and not cause her to stir, I creep out the door and close it silently.

I have a vague, silly idea of where I'm going. I realize that last night at the séance, or whatever it was, someone was trying to scare me. I haven't told anyone on this ship about Tony or how he died, which means someone must have Googled him or me. The shooting of a police officer had been in all the papers, so it wouldn't be hard to find info, but it also wasn't recent news. And why? Is Grant behind this? Does he know I'm onto his doodles? I need someone to talk to, someone who will help me sort all this out, and who better to wake up in the middle of the night than Dirk? And he's conveniently right down the hall from me.

I tap lightly on the door and wait. He must be sleeping soundly because it doesn't open and I don't hear anything from inside the room. I do, however, hear late night party people leave the elevator, and I don't want to talk to them. They're laughing and jostling each other as they careen down the hall. Doesn't anyone sleep on this ship? It's 3:20 in the morning. This time I use my knuckles on the door, and to me it sounds loud enough to wake everyone on Deck 11. Come on, Dirk!

When he finally opens the door, he's wearing boxer shorts and a puzzled look on his face. Since I'm wearing pajama bottoms and a sweatshirt, there isn't time for a polite explanation. I push past him and say, "Quick! Close the door!" I have an unfair advantage because I'm wide awake. His eyes are heavy with sleep, and he still looks confused.

"Is there something wrong, Julia? Isn't it the middle of the night?"

"It sure is, and since you're wide awake, too, I thought we could chat."

"Right now? Can't it wait until morning?"

"I don't think so." My body suddenly begins to shake, and I try to hide it by wrapping my arms around my stomach. "I don't think I want to be alone."

"But you're not alone. Isn't Olivia with you?"

"Can we please talk?" Tears threaten to spill out of my eyes. Fortunately, Dirk finally notices my distress and says, "Of course, we can." He looks around the room. "Where do you want to sit?"

Without answering, I climb into the bed and get under the covers. I'm not too upset to notice the bed is still warm and smells like his aftershave. When he stands there looking at me, I say, "Well, come on. I don't have all day."

"You're a strange woman, Julia Greene," he says as he joins me in bed. "Strange, but certainly not boring."

Once we settle ourselves, which involves a bit of pillow adjustments and several "Sorry, I didn't mean to poke you," I tell him about the séance, Madam L'Oeil, and the appearance of my deceased husband.

"It's upset me more than I imagined," I say. "I know someone is trying to scare me, but why? And who is this L'Oeil person? Surely that's not her real name. I know she's a phony, and I hate it that she talked about Tony."

When I start to cry, he puts his arm around me, and since that feels really good, I snuggle against him, and one thing leads to another and pretty soon it's 5:00 a.m., and I have a silly grin on my face. So does he.

Dirk gives me a kiss and says, "Why don't you go back to your room and put some clothes on? They'll begin serving early breakfast at 6:00. We can get some coffee and talk some more."

"And get some food," I add. "I've worked up quite an appetite."

It takes me fifteen minutes to get dressed, comb my hair, swipe on some lip gloss, and grab my laptop. I find Dirk sitting at a table outside on the deck, and there are two steaming cups of coffee in front of him. For a while, we sit in silence enjoying the brisk morning air and the lack of people. I open my laptop and find an email from Lescano Ceballo, the art professor at Columbia.

My dear Julia,

How wonderful to hear from you! I've often wondered where you were and what you were doing. Did you go to Egypt? If so, it must have been fascinating. Cecelia and I are retired now and living in Bar Harbor. You may recall I mentioned our summer home there several times.

Now, to your question about the Picasso doodles. I don't know under what circumstances you found these, but I sincerely hope you didn't purchase any. They are forgeries—and not very good ones at that. People intent upon forging art often believe Picasso's line drawings are easy targets because they are just that—simple line drawings—but they couldn't be more mistaken. It is extremely difficult to successfully copy the movement, flow, and magic of a Picasso line. The drawings in the photos you sent were done by an amateur—someone who knows very little about art and was therefore unable to understand the complexities of the great artist's line drawings. If you have them in your possession, I suggest you dispose of them immediately. They are of no value.

I hope all is well with you and you are enjoying a happy career in the art field. You were one of my most promising students.

Cecelia also sends best wishes.

Warm regards,

Lescano Ceballo

I pass the laptop to Dirk. "Have a look at this. It proves the doodles are forgeries. Lescano Ceballo is an expert on Picasso's work. If he says they're fake, they are. This has to be the reason Sean is on the ship." A thought occurs to me. "Maybe the doodles aren't the only forgeries. What if there are more? The snake oil salesman has to know about this. I think we should confront him."

"And say what? We know you're selling forgeries and you have to stop? I think we should wait until we dock in Seattle. We can alert the authorities there."

"That's a lame plan. He could be off the ship and gone before the police can arrest him."

He puts his hand over mine. "Listen, Julia, you're still understandably upset, so let's do first things first. We need to find this Madam L'Oeil. Someone put her up to talking about Tony, and we have to find out who it was."

My insides still quiver every time I think about last night. "What about Sean? I'm sure all of this has something to do with him. These people, whoever they are, have stashed him away somewhere. I'm just hoping he's still alive." I pause. "I'm remembering something. Sean told us he had originally intended to come on this cruise with his son. But in the photo he has two little daughters. There was no boy. Why would he lie?"

"Maybe he has a son from another marriage," Dirk says. "Or maybe he didn't want to share personal information with strangers. If he is onboard for his job, he would have to keep his identity secret, so it stands to reason he'd have a cover story. Did he tell you anything about his work?"

"No, now that I think about it, he didn't. I think he said he was from the Midwest, but that wouldn't be true either."

"We'll figure it out. In the meantime, stop worrying."

"That's what people say when they don't have the answers," I mumble.

"Excuse me?"

"I said I'm hungry. Let's get breakfast."

CHAPTER SEVENTEEN

"This thing with the medium concerns me," Dirk says. "This L'Oeil or whatever her name is was trying to send you a warning. Is someone putting her up to it? Or is she somehow involved in the forged doodles and missing passenger? We need to find out."

He and I are down on Deck 5 in front of Madam L'Oeil's door. Just standing there is making my stomach hurt. I don't want to see her or the room ever again.

"There's no point in trying to confront her," I mumble. "She'll just deny it or say her snow globe isn't talking."

He arches his eyebrows. "Her snow globe?"

"Yes, she uses it to contact spirits. They come from the Other Side into the globe and tell her they're ready to work."

"Sorry I asked. We're going to get this sorted, out and then you're going to take a long nap."

"What are you going to say?" I whisper. "What if she won't talk to you?"

"She'll talk. You forget I'm a lawyer. I know how to intimidate people."

He knocks on the door, and I resist the urge to hide behind him. His face looks stern, and I'm pretty sure I'd be afraid of him if I didn't know him. The door opens a crack, and a short, dark-haired woman peers out.

"Is she the one?" he says in my ear. I shake my head.

"We're looking for Madam L'Oeil. I understand this is her cabin.

"No one here," the woman says in a low voice, putting a finger to her lips.

"I'm sure we have the right room. Can you tell us where we can find her?"

"No Madam L'Oeil here." Again with the finger to the lips. The woman is beginning to look agitated, but Dirk remains stern.

"May we step in and look around?"

"Dirk," I say putting a hand on his arm, "maybe we shouldn't hassle her. She doesn't understand us, and she looks pretty scared."

But he's already in the room, and I'm right behind him. It looks the same as last night, but the table with the snow globe is gone, and in its place is a Pack and Play—with a baby in it. There's also a stack of diapers on the bed, along with baby clothes and cans of formula.

The woman is young, perhaps not yet twenty, but the black shirt and pants she is wearing make her look older. She stands protectively in front of the Pack and Play twisting her hands nervously.

"Bambina."

"Yes." I smile. "I can see that. What is her name?"

"Scusa?"

"Her name? Nome?"

Her face lights up. "Sophia."

"Sophia. That's a very pretty name." I point to her. "And your name?"

"Isabella."

"Also very pretty. Isabella, we're looking for the lady who was here last night. Do you know where she is?"

I see the confused look on her face and realize I've exhausted her English vocabulary. As I search for more words, my eyes fall on a framed photograph on the table. It's of a smiling man with dark hair and a moustache wearing a Golden Eagle crew uniform holding a baby. I've seen that man before, and he wasn't wearing a uniform or smiling. Because when I saw him, he was dead. That's the man I saw in the morgue. I point to the photo and say to Isabella, "Who is this? Is this your husband?"

"Si." Tears well in her eyes. "Mio marito è morto."

I give the picture to Dirk. "I don't know much Italian, but I'm pretty sure she said her husband is dead. This is the man I saw in the morgue—the one who supposedly fell onto a lifeboat. Remember I told you that seemed suspicious because there was no blood or crushed bones on the body."

His stunned expression surprises me. "I'm pretty sure you never told me about your visit to the morgue. I don't think I'd have forgotten that."

"Well, it doesn't matter now. We have to find out what happened, but I don't think she'll be able to tell us."

Isabella looks so young and scared, and I wish with all my heart I could comfort her, but my Italian is limited to *arrivederci* and *molto beni,* neither of which will be helpful in this situation. I do, however, know someone who may be able to help. But right now I need to talk to Melissa.

She is sampling perfumes in a shop on Deck 7. When she spots Dirk and me, she turns the atomizer our way and sprays, sending a heavy, cloyingly sweet cloud in our direction. Dirk manages to duck, but it catches me squarely in the face.

"Isn't that divine?" she asks. "I think I'm going to buy this."

"Swell." My throat feels like it's closing, but I manage to say, "Can I talk to you for a minute?"

"Only for a minute. I have to go to yoga. Isn't this cruise wonderful? Did you enjoy last night? Too bad no one connected with the spirits. What in the world was up with Phoebe? She seemed very upset."

When she finally winds down, I say, "I need to find this Oeil person. How can I reach her?"

She dabs more of the fragrance on her wrists. "I told you I overheard her talking to a passenger on deck, and I asked her then to do our séance. I have no idea how to get in touch with her."

A thought occurs to me. "How was she dressed when you saw her? She surely wasn't wearing her turban and long skirt."

Melissa frowns. "As I recall it was misting that day. She was wearing some kind of rain hat and a plastic raincoat. Why all the questions? Do you need her services?"

"I just want to ask her if she found my pen. I think I left it in her room."

"Why don't you go to her room and ask her?"

"I did. She's not there."

"Can't you buy another one in the shop?"

"I could, but the one I'm looking for is a Mont Blanc. I don't think they sell them here, nor do I want to pay for a new one."

She needs to stop asking questions because lying is exhausting and I'm running out of fibs. Fortunately, she turns her attention back to perfume. "Sorry I can't help you, Julia. Maybe you should ask at the front desk."

A good idea. Why didn't I think of that?

The person behind the desk, a bespectacled man named Krim, who's wearing a black vest and pants, folds his hands into a teepee and asks for the name of the guest. He has a very strong Baltic accent but seems to understand me. When I tell him what I want, he consults his computer then shakes his head and says, "We have no passenger with the name of Madame

L'Oeil. Would she perhaps have another name, madam?"

"You mean perhaps Madame something else?"

"Yes, madame, surely."

"I don't think her name is Madame Surely. Maybe Madame something else."

"No, madame. There is no Madame Something Else."

"I know there's no Madame Something Else. I mean Madame some other name. Is there a Madam anything?"

Krim looks like he's going to cry. Dirk puts his arm around my shoulder and says, "Come on, Julia. Let's not bother the nice man any longer. He doesn't know where this Oy person is."

I'm not yet ready to leave. I lean across the counter. "Could you tell me who's in room E685 on Deck 5?"

He seems relieved to hear a question he can answer. "That's easy, madame. That room is reserved for the crew. Will that be all, Madame?"

"Just about," I reassure him. "One more thing. A friend of mine, Sean Mauer, thinks he may have lost his Port Pass a few days ago. He was just wondering if his travel companion had requested a new one." This sounds lame even to my ears, but I'm hoping we have Krim so confused he won't notice the odd question.

"He must report it. Let me see." He once again consults his computer. "I'm sorry, madame, Mr. Mauer has not requested a new Port Pass. Perhaps he found the missing one."

Dirk practically drags me away. "Come on. Let's get a Bloody Mary and forget all about Madame L'Oeil for a minute."

Two Bloody Marys fail to sooth my jitters. All they're doing is giving me a headache. Dirk means well, and I know he's trying to help, but sitting around drinking alcohol isn't helping anything. I need action. And I also think I need to be by myself for a bit, and I don't want to hurt Dirk's feelings.

"I think I'll jog around the deck," I tell him. "Release all those endorphins. Should be good for me."

His face is full of concern. "Are you okay, Julia?"

I'm trying to sound rational, but my mind is spinning like a top. Where on earth is Madame L'Oeil and how was she able to use the room on Deck 5? And what happened to Isabella's husband? If I'd known I'd meet his widow and little daughter, I'd have inspected his body more carefully. I close my eyes and try to remember what I saw. His eyes were closed, and he was fully dressed. There was definitely no sign of a crushed body or congealed blood. I wonder if his body is still in the morgue.

Dirk's voice pulls me out of my thoughts. "You're awfully quiet. What are you thinking about?"

I gaze out at the water and for a few minutes can't speak. When I do, I say, "Something terrible is happening on this ship. I watch all the people laughing and drinking and having a good time, and I want to yell, 'Hey, you all. A man is missing, you're paying for forgeries in the art gallery, another man is dead, and someone is trying to hurt me. Have a good cruise.'"

He puts his arm around me and strokes my hair as if he's calming an upset puppy. I'm waiting for him to tickle me under the chin. "You need to take a break from all this. Why don't you go to your room and lie down?"

I pull away from him. "I don't want to lie down. I want to get some answers. Either I get some answers, or I'm going to explode—so don't try to calm me down. I'll figure out what's going on by myself."

He tries to reason with me, but I'm way beyond that. I feel my face flame as I stalk away. I know I'm being irrational, but I left rational behavior behind days ago. I need to find Sean Mauer. I need to find Madam L'Oeil. I need to find out what happened to Isabella's husband. Maybe what I really need is to find some strong medication.

I walk around the deck thinking about events since we boarded the Golden Eagle. The ship stops—yes, it did in spite of what the dining room steward said. Sean disappears—and I know he did in spite of people telling me he's shacked up with a woman or still in Ketchikan. A man is found dead on top of a lifeboat and the official explanation is he jumped—in spite of showing absolutely no signs of broken bones or blood. Then we have forged Picasso doodles, a medium who knows details about Tony, and multiple attempts to scare the pants off me. I need to go home and forget all this. But first things first.

CHAPTER EIGHTEEN

A few days ago, I heard Rebecca MacPherson speaking Italian to one of the crew, and from the way they laughed and waved their arms around, I figured she was fairly fluent. Now all I have to do is find her. Ten minutes later I'm outside on the Promenade Deck searching for the naturalist.

I see her in the bow of the ship talking to two passengers. She has binoculars around her neck and an annoyed expression on her face.

"I'm sorry you find the food unsatisfactory," I hear her say. "Perhaps you could bring your complaints to the attention of the dining room steward. I'm actually not a crewmember. I'm the naturalist—the one who explains the wonderful wildlife you see on this trip. I have nothing to do with the food."

The man, a loud person wearing shorts, a tank top, flip flops, and a New York accent says, "You're still working on this damn boat, aren't you? Seems to me you should be able to tell our problem to someone. The scrambled eggs we ordered this morning were cold. COLD! There's no excuse for that."

I have to admire Rebecca. She is remaining calm, but I'm imagining I see smoke coming out of her ears.

"I'm sorry, sir, but I honestly can't help you. Take your complaints to the dining room. Or perhaps to the front desk." She looks over the man's head and sees me for the first time. "Julia! Is it already time for our appointment? I'll be right with you."

I immediately understand and play along. "Great, Rebecca. I really need to talk to you." And I'm not just saying that for the couple's benefit. I really do need to talk to her.

She smiles at the upset couple. "Will you please excuse me? I hope you find a solution to your problem."

The man and woman give me a snarky look and walk away, grumbling loudly. Rebecca looks relieved. "Let's go somewhere without people. I can't stand another conversation like that. Don't know what I have to do to convince people I'm not part of the crew."

A private talk suits me perfectly. I sure don't want anyone to overhear us.

The only place I can think of where we won't be interrupted is my stateroom. Once there, we go out to the veranda and, being a good host, I offer my guest a beverage. We have water, which she accepts. She takes a sip and looks at me questioningly.

"Rebecca," I begin, "didn't I once hear you speaking Italian? I'm pretty sure I did because I couldn't understand a word you were saying."

"That's an odd question. I do speak a little. Why do you ask?"

I quickly explain about meeting Isabella and the baby and the photo of the dead husband. I can't mention anything about my visit to the morgue or my suspicions that his death might not have been accidental, so I say, "I'd love to help her with some things for the baby but don't know what she needs or would like. I'm wondering if you'd be willing to come with me and talk to her. She seems so young and scared." Maybe when we actually meet we can work "cause of death" into the conversation. Rebecca's next remark makes me feel like a complete louse. She's being helpful, and I'm calculating a way to get information.

"That is so sweet of you. Of course, I'd be happy to help. Did you know one of the shops on the Promenade Deck has baby clothes? It would be fun to shop for the little one."

I try to ignore my conscience as I say, "Could you come with me right now? I know Isabella is in the room."

Rebecca looks at her watch. "I have an hour before my next lecture. Let's do it."

On the way to Deck 5 we stop at the shop with baby clothes and buy a soft, stuffed whale with plastic eyes that spin and a cute onesie with sailboats on the front.

Isabella is surprised to see us, but Rebecca smiles, says something in Italian, Isabella smiles and says something, and we are in the room. We break the ice by showing her the little onesie and whale and judging from the number of *grazie moltos*, I'm assuming she likes our gifts.

She and Rebecca sit on the couch and begin to chat, and since I don't understand a word they're saying, I wander around the room looking at things.

Sophia is asleep in the Pack and Play. She looks angelic. One small fist is curled against her cheek and a chubby little leg pokes out from under her blanket. I notice more photos of Isabella and Sophia, Sophia and her father, and Isabella and her husband. They look so young and so in love.

Rebecca and Isabella seem to be getting along splendidly. The young mother is even laughing at something Rebecca says. I can't wait to hear what she's learned.

Forty minutes later, Rebecca gets to her feet, hugs Isabella, and blows a kiss to Sophia. As Isabella walks us to the door, I write my cell phone number on a paper and hand it to her.

"If you need anything, please call me. I really mean it." Rebecca translates, which earns me a hug and more *grazie moltos*. Her reaction overwhelms me, and I realize I have tears in my eyes as we leave the room.

I wipe them away and turn to Rebecca. "So what did she say?"

"What a lovely young woman. I feel so sorry for her."

"I do, too. What did she say?"

Rebecca sighs. "It's a sad story. She's been married to her husband, Antonio Romano, for a little over a year. They are both from Sicily and were very excited when he was hired as a crewmember on the Golden Eagle. This was his first trip, and they were having a belated honeymoon. She traveled to Ketchikan to meet the ship when it docked in port and intended to stay with him until they reached Juneau. On the day Antonio died, he'd been working on Deck 9. Isabella wasn't sure what he was doing there. Anyway, she was confused when they told her he had jumped from an upper deck because he had absolutely no reason to commit suicide—they were very happy—and he had never been to the upper decks. He was a very junior crewmember and performed mostly menial chores on the lower decks. I'm afraid she doesn't believe he jumped."

"I knew it! He couldn't have jumped. His body didn't have any blood or bones sticking out."

Rebecca stops walking and looks at me oddly, and I know I've made a mistake. "I mean, that's what I heard from people who saw the body." I quickly change the subject. "And Madam L'Oeil? What did she say about her?"

"I'm getting to that. After Antonio died, they brought a new crewmember on in Skagway, and they needed Antonio's bed, so they offered Isabella the room we just left. She said Antonio's body is still onboard, and she intends to accompany it back to Italy. They are taking the body to Seattle for examination and then will release it to Isabella. She also said the cruise line has been extremely nice to her."

I'll bet it has been, I thought. They don't want her asking questions. "So she has no idea who this L'Oeil is?"

"Nope, but she thinks she must be part of the crew. Otherwise she couldn't have used the room. She said the crew's activity director occasionally scheduled fun events for the crew. She remembered hearing Antonio talk about a fortuneteller or a gypsy who read Tarot cards. Too bad you can't go down to the crew quarters, but that part of the ship is off limits to passengers."

"Yes, it is too bad. I can't thank you enough, Rebecca, and I won't hold you up any longer. Have a good lecture. We'll catch up later."

I hope she can't see how eager I am to get away.

CHAPTER NINETEEN

Since I now know the story of Isabella and Antonio, I feel I owe it to the young mother to go back to the morgue and have another look at the body, and I don't want to go by myself. I also know Olivia is going to be resistant to my plan, so I don't tell her what I'm up to until we're on the elevator on the way to Deck 6.

"All you have to do is distract the nurse if she's in there. I'll swipe the key and we'll be on our way."

Olivia neatly folds the ship newspaper she'd been reading and tucks it in her tote bag. "The Fancy Dress Ball is coming up. We should probably be thinking about costumes. Sorry. I guess I haven't been paying attention. Where are we going? And what key do you intend to swipe?"

"I just want another peek at the body."

She stops applying lip gloss and stares at me. "What body? What on earth are you talking about? Honestly, Julia, I wish I knew how your mind works. I'm not saying it's not interesting. All I'm saying is a heads up would be nice."

"I need to see Antonio's body one more time—just to make sure I'm right. I don't think he committed suicide. I think he was somehow murdered."

The expression on her face is hard to read. Olivia is used to my...ah...creative ideas, but I don't think she saw this one coming. She basically looks upset.

"Okay, let me get this straight. I'm going to help you get the key to the morgue. And after that what are we doing?"

I swallow hard. "Well, I'm hoping you'll help me examine the body and confirm my theory."

She's silent from Deck 10 to Deck 4. When the door opens, she steps out, puts her hands on her hips, and glares at me. "I don't understand how you can function so nicely as a business woman in North Carolina and go completely off the rails on what is supposed to be a relaxing vacation. This is the second time."

I know she's referring to our trip to Iceland and the murder of one of our group there, but she has to admit none of that was my fault. But she does have a point. If I hadn't become worried about Sean Mauer's disappearance, chances are we'd be sipping mimosas on the veranda and letting the world float by. But I did, and there's no going back now.

"Come on, Olivia, a little baby has no father due to what I suspect is foul play. We have to try to find out what happened."

"What is it you want me to do?"

Hooray! She's in! "Get the nurse out of the way. Do you have any rashes she could look at or maybe fake a sore throat?"

"I'll think of something," she mutters as we push open the door and walk in. This time there are other passengers waiting to see the doctor, so we sit and fidget until the other patients are gone and it's finally Olivia's turn. I pretend to read a magazine while my friend explains her symptoms to the nurse. She must have been convincing because she gives me a thumbs up as she follows the nurse to an exam room. As the waiting room is empty, I quickly dart around the counter, snatch the key from the board, and stick it in my pocket. I'm pacing around the hall when Olivia finally returns.

"The nurse said I have rhinitis. I think that means a drippy nose. I didn't even know I was sick. She gave me nose drops, a decongestant, and throat lozenges."

I clap my hands. "See! This is a good thing." I look at her as appealingly as I can. "Won't you please come with me and have a look at the body? I promise it won't take long."

She chews on her lower lip and doesn't look happy. "Let's clear up a few details. How do you propose to return the key? I'm not going back in there."

"No problem. I'm going to drop it in the hall somewhere. They'll think they lost it."

"A half-baked plan." But she comes with me when I unlock the door.

It's cold in the room, and Antonio is no longer on the table in front of the drawers. I try to push out of my mind the thought of what the body must be like by now. I'm hoping the drawers are refrigerated. I tentatively open one and am relieved to see it's cold enough in there to freeze beef. This one is empty.

Olivia is getting bolder by the minute. "Try the next one. This isn't so bad."

The next one holds Antonio. I pull out the tray and quickly realize he isn't wearing any clothes.

"Boy, things do shrink when you're dead," Olivia says as she observes the body.

I'm not interested in shrunken body parts. I'm looking for any signs of death due to plunging downward from a great height. But there's nothing. His arms and legs don't appear to be broken, his neck isn't hanging at an impossible angle, and there are no bruises. I can't see the back of his head, and even I am too squeamish to lift it up for a look.

Olivia has also been giving the body a visual once over. "I think you're right. It doesn't look like he fell.

Did you see this?" She points to a toe tag on his foot. "Cause of death. Suspicious drowning."

I'm very confused. If Antonio drowned, why were we told he jumped to his death? Did this drowning happen the night we sailed from Ketchikan, which was the night the ship stopped? And which was also the day Sean disappeared. I push the tray back in and close the drawer. "Let's get out of here. I've got what I came for."

I open the door, scan the hallway, and seeing it empty, we bolt out of the morgue. I drop the key on the floor and run to the elevator.

"I'm convinced his death wasn't accidental," I tell Dirk. We're sitting in the Pelican Lounge having cake and coffee. I've selected a German Kirsch Kuchen and am torn between eating and talking.

"Here's how I see it. Remember when the ship stopped even though everyone swears it didn't? I think that's when they found Antonio. He saw something or knew something and that's when someone pushed him overboard. I don't know how they got him out of the water—maybe they even tried to rescue him, but it was too late." I pause for a bite of delicious chocolate and cherries. "That's also when Sean disappeared and the captain made that announcement. You know, the more I think about it, the captain probably has no idea what's going on. This is a huge ship with over fifteen hundred crew members. He probably isn't bothered with every little thing that happens and relies on others to handle problems."

Dirk hasn't touched his lemon cream pie. "You could be right. A message probably has to go through a lot of people before it gets to him. But he did make that cryptic announcement. He had to know something was going on."

As we talk, I spot Grant Merino coming across the deck. He sees us and stops to chat. Knowing what I do about the doodles, I'm afraid to look the art director in the eye. Dirk shoots me a warning glance, which I know means not to blurt out everything I know.

"Are you all coming to the art auction?" Grant asks. "We have some nice pieces coming up."

"Any Picasso doodles?" What is wrong with me? I try to ignore Dirk's unsubtle kick under the table.

The art director swings his eyes to mine. "Certainly, if you're interested. Are you?"

"Maybe. I'm worried about the authenticity." Am I imagining it, or has his expression hardened?

"I told you before, that isn't a worry. Everything can be authenticated."

Dirk abruptly stands up. "Come on, Julia. I just remembered it's time for our couples massage. You'll excuse us, won't you, Grant?"

We're almost to our room before Dirk speaks. "Honestly, Julia, one of these days you're going to get yourself into real trouble. Why did you have to bait him? Now he's probably thinking we're on to him."

"Well, we are."

"Yes, I know that, but we don't have to let him know."

"Sorry. My bad." But I'm not really listening to him. I'm thinking how nice a couple's massage would be.

CHAPTER TWENTY

Phoebe Skofield is sitting by herself outside in a deck chair. In spite of the blanket wrapped around her, she's shivering. Her chin is propped in her hand, and she's staring out at the water. She doesn't notice me standing in front of her until I cough softly. When she looks up, I see she's crying.

"I don't mean to bother you," I say. "I'll go away if you want me to."

She uses the back of her hand to brush tears off her face. "Don't go. I need to talk to someone, and you were at that awful séance."

I sit down beside her and stretch out my legs. "It was, indeed, terrible. How did that phony medium get her info? I'd love to know who fed her all that stuff. I've looked all over the ship for her. Do you have any idea who she is?"

Phoebe shakes her head. "I don't believe she was talking to the dead, but I can't figure out how she knew all those details either." Tears welled up in her eyes again.

"I don't mean to be intrusive," I say, "but did she know accurate facts about your life? She sure did about mine. Remember the man she said wanted to speak to someone in the room? I think she was talking about my deceased husband. I was shocked—and very distressed."

Phoebe's tears keep coming. I find some clean tissue in my pocket and offer it to her.

"I'm assuming you have a similar story?"

She doesn't realize she's ripping the tissue to shreds. "That medium is so hateful. It was one of the worst moments in my life, and how she could know about it is beyond me."

I wait for her to say more.

"She was talking about my baby. Her name was Sarah. And the woman was my mother. They were both killed in a car accident. My dad and I survived. I had her when I was seventeen, and the father disappeared before she was born. We were from a very small town in Ohio, and my mother never got over the scandal of an illegitimate granddaughter."

I reached over and took her hand. "I'm so sorry, Phoebe. It must have hurt you soul to hear this woman talk about your family. Tell me, who else knows about this?"

"Nobody. I certainly haven't told anyone on this ship. I suppose someone could Google it because the accident was in the paper, but why do that? I wasn't married then, so they would also have to know my maiden name. What about you?"

"My husband was a cop, and he was murdered one night trying to stop a robbery." I gulp. "He was shot through the heart. One bullet, and he was dead,"

"That's terrible," Phoebe murmurs. "How awful for you." Her tears are gone and she looks indignant. "Who is this person? And why is she doing it?"

"I don't know, but I sure am trying to find out. Phoebe, do you know of anyone who would want to hurt you? Or know anyone who might have fed this information to the Madam L'Oeil?"

"No, and it won't do any good to go looking for her. I already tried that. No one has ever heard of her. There's one thing, though…"

"What? Do you have an idea about who she might be?"

"No, but I think she was wearing a wig. We were the first ones to arrive for the séance, and I saw the fake medium standing at a mirror straightening it." She smiles. "I think the hair was attached to the turban."

"Come to think of it, you might be right. I thought her hair looked too black to be real."

Her face lights up when she sees Martin, her husband, coming toward us. "Please don't tell him I told you about Sarah. He's still so angry at this person. He even went to the front desk and complained, but they said they'd never heard of her. The man at the desk did say that room was reserved for ship personnel. Do you suppose she's a member of the crew? If she is, we'll never find her."

I'm not so sure about that. As she talks, I get an idea.

"So it's basically playing dress up," I tell Olivia. "We'll disguise ourselves and have a look. A very fast scouting expedition, and no one will recognize us."

"Where is this scouting expedition going to be?" We're in a shop specializing in costumes for the Golden Eagle Fancy Dress Ball, which will happen tomorrow night. Olivia holds up a sequined gold lamé sheath flashy enough to be seen in Seattle. "I might rent this for the ball, although it smells of cheap perfume."

"I was thinking we could go to the crew's quarters and see if we can find Madam L'Oeil." Before Olivia can object, I say, "It will be perfectly safe because we'll be disguised."

I'm expecting outrage, but instead I get a deep sigh. "I know you're upset about that person implying she was talking to Tony, so we do need to find her. I feel I'm obligated to keep you from tossing her overboard."

As we talk, I'm looking through a rack of all kinds of costumes—princess, vampire, clown, nurse, and— whoa—a fortune teller. And it's exactly like the one

Madam L'Oeil wore. I pull it off and hold it up in front of Olivia.

"Where have you seen this before?" It's a cream-colored, off-the-shoulder blouse, wide olive-green belt, and full red and cream skirt. The black high-heeled boots are placed neatly under the rack.

"It sure looks like the outfit she was wearing. Do you suppose she rented it here?"

"There's only one way to find out." I wait until the salesperson finishes with a customer and then ask her about the costume. "A lovely lady was wearing this at a party the other night. She forgot to pick up the photos she'd taken, and we'd like to make sure she gets them. Unfortunately, she left so quickly we didn't get her name. Could you possibly tell us who rented it?"

The woman is busy folding Spiderman T-shirts. "I have no idea. I've had the last two days off."

At least this woman speaks and understands English. Her accent sounds German.

"Would you have a record of the rental?"

"No, all we care about is that the article of clothing is returned. If it's badly damaged or not returned at all, we can charge the Port Pass. Otherwise you just select what you want, show us your Port Pass, and take the costume to your room. No charge if it comes back in good condition."

"Then you must have the Port Pass number," I say.

She frowns. "Once the article is returned, we erase the transaction. There's no reason to keep it."

She returns to the T-shirts, and I turn to Olivia. "So now we know Madam L'Oeil wore a costume. Let's look through the wigs and see what we find."

There are six shelves full of wigs, but I don't see a turban with black hair. Olivia pulls a blonde curly wig over her auburn hair and looks in the mirror. "I think blonde hair suits me. I look quite different."

She looks great. The blonde hair goes perfectly with her olive skin, but as I said before, she'd look good with a bag over her head. I try a platinum wig styled in a short bob and show it to Olivia.

"That makes you look kind of pasty. I mean, the wig is almost white, and your skin is pretty pale. You need something with a bit more pizazz." She hands me a sleek, shoulder-length black wig with bangs. "That's much better. A bit of eyebrow pencil, some mascara, and no one will recognize you."

We look through the costumes and try on the nurse uniforms, but they make us both look like aging hookers. Olivia's is too short and doesn't cover all the pertinent lower areas, and I look just plain silly. We decide to dress from our own wardrobes as closely as we can to resemble the crew uniform. Fortunately, we both have black skirts and white blouses and white sneakers. We also decide not to rent costumes for the Fancy Dress Ball. We'll wear our own evening gowns and carry masks that Olivia and I will create. We should look splendid—and, above all, won't smell like cigarettes, sweat, and cheap perfume.

CHAPTER TWENTY-ONE

"Hello Julia,

How interesting to hear you have a degree in art history. It would be fun to talk to you someday. Edward Hopper is one of my favorite artists, too. And how great to hear you're cruising to Alaska on the Golden Eagle.

I feel as if I'm getting to know you, so would you mind if I ask you for a small favor? My husband is on your cruise—or at least he's supposed to be. I haven't heard from him since the ship sailed and I am becoming a bit worried. His name is Sean Mauer. Do you suppose you could inquire at the desk if he is indeed onboard? I would be so grateful.

Best,

Courtney"

I've been waiting for this email, and now that it's come, I don't know how to reply. I don't want to alarm this nice woman, but maybe if she knows Sean is missing, she can tell me something to help find him.

Hi Courtney,

I'm not sure how to go about saying this. Your husband is on the ship, I have met him, and he's an extremely nice man. My friend and I were with him on the group tour to Potlatch Park, and we all enjoyed talking to him. In fact, so much so that we—several of us—had arranged to meet for a pre-dinner drink in a lounge. (I say "several of us" so she doesn't think there was any fooling around between her husband and me.)

This is the difficult part; he never turned up, and none of us has seen him since. I'm convinced he's onboard because there are cameras all over the decks, and it would be impossible to fall into the water unnoticed. I know that's a scary thing to read, but I'm just trying to give you the facts. I was hoping he had contacted you.
Warmly,
Julia"

"Julia,
What?! What do you mean no one has seen him? He has to be there somewhere. What should I do?
Yours in panic,
Courtney"

"Hey Courtney,
Don't panic. I guess what I was asking is—and this is hard to write—he wouldn't be off with some lady, would he? There are plenty of single women trolling on this ship, and it would be easy for him to disappear into someone's stateroom. I managed to get into his room because I thought he might be sick and unable to call for help. He wasn't there, but I did see the photo of you and your daughters. It had fallen on the floor, and the frame was loose, and the photo had fallen out (a very small untruth, basically to protect the guilty—me). His FBI ID card fell out with it. Was he working on a case on this trip? I know you can't tell me confidential info, but anything you can share would be helpful.
Again, for what it's worth, I'm convinced he's on the ship.
Don't worry,
Julia"

I realize Courtney has no idea who I am. For all she knows, I could be a raving lunatic who has stashed her husband away for my own nefarious purposes.

"Hello, Julia,
I've had a bit of time to think and am not quite sure what to believe. I feel I should alert the ship's authorities about my husband if he is truly missing. One thing is sure, though. I'm not going to reveal any kind of information to you. I don't know you, and I don't know your motive for being involved in this. My husband might be working and is therefore unavailable to contact any of us. Thank you for your concern.
Best,
Courtney Mauer"

Oh my! I can certainly understand Courtney possibly thinking I'm a whacko. Somehow I have to convince her I'm not.

"Hey Courtney,
You are absolutely right to voice your worries. I have an idea. Would it help convince you I'm telling the truth and really do want to help you if I get my good friend, Dirk Harrison, to vouch for me? He's a respected lawyer in Sacramento, California, and you can Google him and read about a big case he just won. He's on this ship and knows all about Sean. Let me know.
Warmly,
Julia"

I don't know how Dirk is going to feel about that, but I'm hoping he'll want to help. Just to make sure, I pull out my phone and text him. Can you come to my room right now? I'm here all by myself.

Within seconds he texts back. *On my way.*

While I wait for Courtney to reply, I pace around the room. For some reason, there are two dark chocolate candy bars on the sink in the bathroom. They shouldn't be there, so I eat them. Now I'm really thirsty, so I drink some water straight out of the tap. You're not supposed to do that so I gargle with mouthwash. I'm hunting for something savory to counteract all the sugar when Dirk arrives.

"What's up, cupcake? I got here as fast as I could." He envelopes me in a satisfying hug, which I'd like to prolong, but first things first. I show him the emails from Courtney.

"As you can see, she's a bit skeptical about my motives. I can't say I blame her, but maybe she can tell us something that will help."

"It looks to me as if she's either obtained legal advice or has talked to someone about your emails who has told her to be very careful. It's totally understandable. Under these circumstances, I wouldn't say anything either."

"I know all that, but will you help? All you have to say is Sean hasn't been seen since Ketchikan."

"I can't say I haven't seen him because I've never met the man. Are you absolutely sure he hasn't come back to his room?"

I don't answer right away because I'm remembering the jacket on the bed and the photo on the floor. But I'm convinced Sean didn't move those things, someone else did. I look Dirk in the eye and say, "I'm absolutely sure."

Just at that moment the laptop dings, and there's a message from Courtney.

"Hello Julia,

I've checked Dirk Harrison's credentials and will speak with him if he's available. I'm just hoping you all are who you say you are.
Courtney"

"Hey, Courtney,
Great! Dirk is here—and to prove it, here's a photo. I grab a copy of the ship's paper dated today, hold it in front of Dirk and me, and take a selfie. Dirk looks like a startled deer, but he resembles his Google photo, and it doesn't matter what I look like. Does this convince you?
Julia"

"Julia,
It does. Let me talk to Mr. Harrison.
Courtney"

I hand the laptop to Dirk and while he chats with Courtney on via email, I search for something else to eat. I tend to eat when I'm nervous. I find a pack of peanut butter crackers in my backpack and a small bag of pretzels saved from the flight to Seattle. I'm rummaging through Olivia's tote bag looking for something edible when Dirk says, "Okay, we're done."

I plop down next to him on the bed. "So what did she say? Does she know anything?"

"She said her husband was on the cruise for business. If it had been for pleasure, she would have joined him. She doesn't know exactly what he was doing, but his last few jobs have dealt with stolen art."

"I knew it," I yell. "He discovered the fake doodles. And maybe more. I'll bet Grant Merino knows where Sean is."

"Slow down. That's pure speculation. For the record, she also said she didn't believe her husband would have gone off with another woman. She said he wasn't that kind of a man." He sees my face and says, "I know, I know, but you yourself said he seems like a decent man. I must admit I'd like to know what's happened to him."

I rub my hands together. "Oh boy! We've got a murder, a missing man, and fake art. I'll bet they're all connected."

"Why don't we stop talking for awhile." He puts his arm around me. "It isn't often we're alone."

Okay. I can do that.

CHAPTER TWENTY-TWO

Olivia is lying on the bed with a wet washcloth on her forehead. She has what she is now calling "my sinus headache." Ever since the nurse in the infirmary told her she has rhinitis, she's been shooting salt water up her nose and drinking enormous amounts of "vitamin water." I have no idea what's in vitamin water, but it certainly makes her pee a lot. This is all very annoying because she felt fine before her visit to the infirmary, and now we spend an inordinate amount of time looking for restrooms.

I lift the washcloth off her face and say, "Do you want to go buy decorations to make our masks for the Fancy Dress Ball? If we're actually going to create them ourselves, we should get going."

"Making masks sounds like too much work."

"Right. Then we can rent them at the costume store. We can probably find some that weren't used by smokers."

She tosses the washcloth on the floor and gets off the bed. "You win. Where do we buy the stuff we need?"

"Come with me and I'll show you. If we get started now, we'll be done in no time. This will be fun."

Olivia slings her bag over her shoulder. "No, it won't be, but whatever."

I guess several other passengers have the same idea because All Things Crafty is so crowded people are lined up outside the door. Olivia turns around. "This isn't going to work for me. I'll come back later. I'm going to get a latte. You can wait if you want to."

I don't want to wait, but I also don't want a latte. I wander around the deck hoping the crowd at the shop will thin. I duck into a jewelry shop when I see Melissa approaching. She greets Grant Merino at the entrance to the gallery and both go inside. I'd like another look at the doodles, but I don't want to talk to Melissa so I browse in shops until I see her leave. Once in the gallery, I head for the doodles. There are several other passengers looking at the art. I overhear a woman say she would like to speak to the director, so I smile and tell her he's in his office in the back of the gallery. The woman walks to the back of the gallery and quickly returns.

"There's no one back there."

I'm puzzled. "There has to be. I saw him go back there a few minutes ago."

"Well, he's not. If you see him, could you please tell him to hold the clown painting for me? I don't know the name of the painting or the name of the artist, but it will look great above our sofa."

I agree, and as soon as she leaves, I head for the office. He has to be there. He didn't come out, and there's no place else to go.

But he isn't. And this is the second time I've seen him go into his office and disappear. The small desk is still cluttered with papers, there's still framed artwork stacked against the wall, and there's still an overflowing wastebasket—but no art director. There has to be another way out, but that makes no sense. We're on a cruise ship, and there are no secret passageways. At least that's what my head is saying, but my hands are searching the walls for a hidden latch or a swinging door. And good grief! There actually is one.

I push on a section of the wall and it gives way revealing a narrow opening and a flight of steps leading down. Forgetting all about caution or barging into the unknown, I push the wall shut behind me and start down the stairs that are steep and seem to go on forever. My shoes create a loud clanging sound as they strike the metal rungs, which I'm sure everyone on the ship can hear. I go down and down until I'm convinced I have to be way below water level. The steps finally come to an end at a heavy metal door. I push it open and go into a narrow hall, lit by an overhead light bulb. At the end of the hall is another door, and this one is locked. I can hear voices on the other side, which must mean this short hall leads to other parts of the ship. I wonder if all the shops have a secret way to access the crew area. It makes sense. The employees can bring merchandise into the shops without disturbing the passengers on the public decks.

This area contains two lockers, and one of them isn't locked, so I look inside. The interior is deep, and there are several paintings stacked against one side. There is also a manila envelope, which contains about twenty of the Picasso doodles. I pull them out for a better look. They're all signed and are mostly drawings of birds— the forger must have trouble duplicating the more complicated doodles—and they are on two different types of paper: paper napkins and toilet paper. And all the papers have smudges, probably done to convince the buyer Picasso was sitting a restaurant and doodling as he ate. I have to laugh at the toilet paper because I'm pretty sure Parisian toilettes weren't stocked with extra soft three-ply. This stash of doodles proves Grant Merino is up to his crooked eyeballs in fake art.

Reluctantly, I put the envelope back in the locker and leave the door the way I found it. I now know how to locate the secret entrance to the hall, I can find this again when I come back with the authorities. As I'm about to leave, I see an employee ID badge hanging on a ribbon from a hook on the wall. Rosa Rossi is the name on it. I can't read the rest so I have no idea what Rosa does on the ship, but this works for me. I need to get into the crew quarters, and Rosa isn't using her pass at the moment. I tuck it in my pocket and retrace my steps up the stairs and out into the office. A little girl sees me and yells, "Mommy, that lady just came through the wall." I hear the mother say, "Annabelle, I told you not to wander away. Get over here." I wiggle my fingers at the girl and leave the gallery.

Olivia is a bit testy. "Where were you? I finished my latte a long time ago. The craft store is fairly empty now. Shall we go in?"

"You'll never believe what I found. Do you know there's a secret wall with a door and steps that lead to the crew area in the art gallery?"

"Sure there is. Let's get this over with."

The store has an eclectic array of things. The front shelves contain souvenirs and knickknacks, and the back sells material for Fancy Dress accessories. The amount of kitsch astounds me, but I suppose there's something for everyone. I pick up a plastic gold whale with THE GOLDEN EAGLE stamped on the side and wonder how many of these they sell. Olivia, who is ahead of me, suddenly appears.

"Take a look at this. You're not going to believe it." She's holding a snow globe with a naked woman sitting on the ground, and when she shakes it, gold glitter flutters down. On the base are the letters THE GOLDEN EAGLE. Olivia glances at my face. "What's wrong with you? I thought you'd be excited to see this."

"It just proves what we've known all along. Madam L'Oeil was a fake. The whole thing was a setup to scare us. I think I'm getting pretty numb."

She firmly takes my arm and leads me to the back of the store. "Come on. We'll do this fancy dress thing, have one last hooray on the ship, and it will be over. May I just say, however, this hasn't been the most relaxing vacation I've ever had. We are going to have to take a long rest when we get home."

I'm losing my enthusiasm for this project by the minute. Olivia notices and says, "Why are you slumped over the table like that? You're the one who thought this was a great idea."

"It seems so ridiculous to think about fancy dress and masks when there is so much skullduggery on this ship."

"Skullduggery? Honestly, Julia, have you had anything to eat? I think your blood sugar must be low. Come on. Stop mooning about and find something to use for decoration. I'm actually looking forward to wearing my gown. It'll be fun to get all dressed up. We'll stop at the pizza place and fix your empty tummy."

We each buy plastic masks on long sticks. For decoration we purchase lace, glitter, sequins, feathers, and a bottle of glue. Twenty minutes later, armed with four slices of artichoke, red peppers, tomatoes, olives, and mozzarella pizza, we spread our decoration material out on the bed.

"Now I don't want to do this," Olivia says.

I squirt some glue on the mask and sprinkle it with glitter. My finger pokes a hole in the lace, and it tears. Cheap lace. "I don't want to do this either, but I know what I do want to do."

My friend yawns. "I know what you need to do. You need to go home and forget all this intrigue. Get back to good old North Carolina blue skies and fresh air."

"The air isn't fresh in August," I remind her. "It's hot and full of humidity. Don't I recall you saying it's like living in a swamp?" I push the decorations away and say, "Put on your black skirt. And a white shirt. I have a plan."

CHAPTER TWENTY-THREE

We look like hookers. At least Olivia does. Her black skirt couldn't possibly be part of a uniform because it's way too short, and the blonde wig makes her look sexy. I just look strange. My skirt lands at an unattractive length below my knees, and I notice too late that the white shirt has a stain on the front. The bangs on my wig hang down past eyebrows, making vision difficult. I console myself with the thought that no one can possibly recognize us. I pull Rosa's ID badge that I purloined from Grant's office over my head and off we go.

"So what's the plan?" Olivia asks. We're out on deck and standing in front of a roped off stairway that says "Crew Only."

"We wait until there's no one about, and then we go down there. Since this Oeil person was using a room reserved for the crew, I figure she must be down there. I don't expect her to be roaming around dressed as a gypsy, but I'm hoping somehow we'll be able to spot her. And there must be people who know her."

Olivia seems unimpressed. "You realize this is an idiotic plan, don't you? There are over one thousand crewmembers, and they are all probably working now in various parts of the ship. I don't know why I let you talk me into these things."

As we chat, a passenger approaches and hands Olivia his Port Pass. "Could you get us two vodka sodas, please? We're over there in those deck chairs."

I open my mouth to reply in the negative, but Olivia smiles and says, "Certainly, sir."

Before I can say anything, she trots to the nearest bar and soon returns with the drinks. She carefully places them on a table next to the people. "I've brought some mixed nuts, too, in case you want some munchies." The man compliments her on her fluent English, and Olivia almost curtsies as she says, "Thank you, sir. Languages fascinate me. I've tried, how you say, to speak correctly."

"You need to get rid of that smug look on your face," I say when she walks back to me.

"Well, at least we know we look like part of the crew. Now let's get out of here before we have to take more orders. They bartender asked me if I was new and if he could have my room number."

I move the *Crew Only* chain across the steps and hold my breath as Olivia and I quickly descend undetected. When no one shoots us in the back, I run down the steps and into a long, wide hall. The floor and the walls are painted a pristine, gleaming white. The only color comes from announcements, brochures, and photos on bulletin boards on the walls. I'm amazed at the length of the corridor. It seems to go on forever.

"This is called the I-95 on cruise ships," I whisper. "It's basically the main highway through the boat. The crew can access everywhere from here."

I stop talking when three people dressed in black and white come toward us. They are chatting among themselves and barely notice us as they pass, although one of the men gives Olivia a short once over.

I push some of the annoying black fringe out of my face. "I'm feeling much better. Our disguises are working. Now let's see what we can find out."

The crew area isn't as posh and elaborate as the upper decks, but I like it. It smells good, and I soon understand why. We've reached a large room with tables and chairs at one end, and at the far end two chefs wield knives and ladles as they serve food. It looks very casual and inviting and far more appealing than the crowded dining rooms above.

"I could use a little something," Olivia says. "Maybe just a taste of that delicious smelling roast."

"You're kidding! That would really be pushing our luck..." But I'm talking to air. She already has a tray and utensils and is standing in line.

I must admit I'm feeling a bit peckish, too, since we didn't eat the pizza in our room, so I pick up a tray and join her.

She turns around and winks. "Atta girl! Might as well go down together."

But we don't go down. We pile our plates with roast beef, mashed potatoes, gravy, green beans, and applesauce and sit down at a table. Olivia takes a bite of meat and smiles broadly. "Now this is good! Why doesn't our food taste like this?" She points her fork at me. "I'll tell you why. They have roast in the dining rooms, but it's always gooped up with some kind of fancy sauce. This is much better. A bit of horseradish is all it needs."

I'm still too nervous to comment on the food. I'm watching everyone for the slightest indication that someone is on to us. Even as I taste the tiniest bit of creamy mashed potatoes and delectable beans that have been cooked with bacon, I'm watching.

Finally, Olivia sits back and pats her stomach. "Now for a sweet."

"No, we should get out of here."

"Nonsense. I'm going to have a piece of that blueberry cheesecake and some coffee."

"You certainly are not. We can't stay here. I don't want to be put in the brig."

"You worry too much."

I guess I do. She eats a piece of cheesecake and slowly drinks her coffee. By the time she finishes, I've chewed two Tums and am searching my bag for more.

Once again in the hall, we stop to look at the announcements on the bulletin board. "Look here," Olivia says. "Someone is offering Chinese lessons. I wonder how many takers there are for that."

As she talks, I search the notices for anything resembling fortune telling or séances or talks with folks in the Great Beyond, but there's nothing. Olivia links elbows with me and says, "This place is great. It has a very relaxed feeling. I kind of wish we were down here." Before I can stop her, she strolls into a large room with leather couches, big screen TVs on the walls, a pool table, and a bar loaded with liquor bottles. "This must be the party place I've heard about. You can come here if one of the crew brings you. It's awesome."

I want to go. We're going to get caught. I can feel it in my bones. I pull Olivia's arm and try to lead her out, but she isn't finished sightseeing. "Would you look at this. It's a shop especially for the crew. I'm going in.'

Lordy! While Olivia browses, I hang by the entrance, ready for a quick getaway. I try to loiter and avoid the eyes of the girl working the register. I read a sign on the counter that says this is a consignment store for crewmembers. They can sell things here they might have picked up in ports or received as gifts. And on a shelf behind the girl is a very familiar snow globe. I ask to see it, and when she hands it to me, I immediately know this is the one L'Oeil used. The entire base is sticky and has remnants of ripped off tape.

"Excuse me," I say. "could you possibly tell me where this came from? I'm very interested."

The girl does not look interested. "No idea. People bring stuff in here all the time."

Another girl, who's dusting shelves, hears us and comes over. "I think Irina brought it in. I remember because we didn't want to take it. The bottom looks damaged."

I can feel my heart thudding in my chest. "Do you happen to know who Irina is? Or where I could find her?"

She shakes her head. "She's somebody's girlfriend, I think. She's not a crewmember, but she can use the crew quarters. Maybe she's an officer's girlfriend, but that doesn't give her the right to try to give us damaged goods."

"Certainly not," I say, trying to sound as indignant as she does. "In that case, I don't want to buy it."

The girl puts the snow globe back on the shelf. "Wise decision." Her voice drops to a whisper. "You can buy this in a shop on the Promenade Deck. Brand new, and it won't have a messed-up base."

I thank her and motion for Olivia to hurry up. We have to get out of here.

And we almost make it. We're on I-95 heading for the stairs when a voice yells, "Where do you think you're going?"

I look around to see who the recipient of the angry voice might be. A short, bald man wearing a hairnet and sporting a significant pot belly stomps up to us and pokes his finger in my face.

"Let me see your ID."

Now my heart is bouncing around like a basketball in my chest. I'm sure we're on our way to the brig. He glances briefly at my stolen badge and says, "That's what I thought. You shouldn't be wandering around as if you have nothing to do. You'd better get to the kitchen right away."

"Excuse me? I'm not...I don't..."

"You don't know how to get there? You new girls are all alike." He scowls and looks at his watch. "Come on! I'll take you. You're already late for your shift."

"But I..." I look helplessly at Olivia. "My friend here..."

He shifts his eyes to my friend. "Where's your ID? You girls should know better than to roam around without it. There's a fine for that, you know." He jerks his thumb at Olivia. "You come, too. Where are your hairnets?"

Olivia stops. "I'm sorry, but I absolutely refuse to wear a hairnet. It's a very unattractive look."

The man shrugs. "Up to you." He pulls two hairnets out of his pocket. "Wear them or be fired."

Olivia laughs. "You can't fire us. I'll have you know the two of us own a lunchroom in North Carolina and..."

"And I'm the King of England. Get moving. You're lucky I'm not reporting you."

We seem to have no choice. "Shall we make a run for it?" Olivia whispers.

I turn around and look down the hall. If we try to run, the man will start shouting, and shouting will bring more people, and more people will mean we're busted. But so what? We're passengers on a cruise ship, and maybe we're making one tiny mistake by visiting the crew quarters, but what's the worst they can do? Send us back to the upper decks with a gentle warning not to come back here. I'm about to get indignant when I remember the purloined ID badge around my neck. I don't really want to explain that.

Olivia nudges me in the side. "Are you listening to me? What do you think he wants us to do?"

We soon find out. We follow him into a cavernous kitchen and through aisles of gleaming stainless steel appliances and counters. Hanging above the counters are rows of stainless steel pots and ladles. Everything is sparkling clean. I think about our kitchen at Little Bites in Wake Forest. It's not dirty, but I certainly wouldn't lick a counter. The counters in this kitchen look lickable. They must have people scrubbing them all the time.

They do. Olivia and I discover this very quickly. The man points to a sink full of dirty pots and pans and says, "After you finish here, you can wipe down the refrigerators and counters. Where are your hairnets, ladies? I'm not going to tell you again."

Olivia looks at the ID badge on his shirt and says, "Marco, is it? Listen, Marco. These hands don't do dishes—and certainly not without the proper gloves. See these nails? They don't just happen. They cost a fortune, and I don't want any of them chipped or broken."

Marco isn't impressed. "Are you for real? It's against the rules to wear that polish." But he doesn't sound angry, so I figure Olivia's pheromones must have kicked in—even when she's wearing a hairnet. "Just get to work. I don't want to have to report you."

When he's gone, Olivia leans against the sink. "There's no way I'm doing this. Let's get out of here."

But we can't. There are now other women working and chattering all around us. One calls, "Hey, you with the green nails. We need those pots right away."

I look at my friend and shrug. "Coming right up." I stick my hands in the hot soapy water, pick up a dish mop, and go to work. This isn't so bad. I'm actually enjoying it a bit. The sink is stainless steel and as big as a bathtub. The size makes washing much easier, and I wonder how we could get one for Little Bites. Our old porcelain sink is small and tends to fill up with dirty dishes quickly. As I wash, I listen to the voices. Such a jumble of different languages interspersed with bursts of laughter. Several sous chefs are chopping onions, parsley, garlic, and herbs for what I assume will be the base of something tasty. Another stirs an enormous pot of French onion soup with a long wooden spoon. The smells are intoxicating. I lean over to Olivia, who still has a scowl on her face, and say, "Now I understand why there are so many corpulent chefs. Just think what it would be like to inhale all these wonderful aromas all the time."

Her scowl deepens. "It's way too hot in here, and this wig is beginning to make me itch. I can only imagine what it's doing to my hair. Why can't we leave now?"

"We can in a minute. I'm not quite finished with my pans."

"Did I just hear you correctly? You're going to worry about washing these pots? Are you nuts?"

Maybe. I don't know. Probably. I reach for a clean dishtowel and begin to dry the pans. Olivia folds her arms and stares at me, disapproval written all over her face. When the last pot is gleaming, I stack it under the counter and wipe the entire surface with a clean rag. It shines like the rest of them. Now I'm satisfied. I nod to Olivia.

"Time to go. Don't creep away. Walk as if you have a purpose."

It must be shift change now because more people come through the double swinging doors. Everyone is wearing the black-and-white uniforms. The chefs, wearing the traditional toque blanche and white jackets are easy to spot. We are almost to the door when I notice a very tall, very familiar figure in the throng. I stop walking so abruptly Olivia bangs into me. "I can't believe it! Look at that man. Do you recognize him?"

She looks around. "Where? There are a ton of people in here."

"Over there. That tall guy. I think it's Colin Banning."

CHAPTER TWENTY-FOUR

"Why on earth would Colin Banning be part of the crew? This just doesn't make any sense."

Olivia and I make it out of the crew quarters without being stopped and have ditched our black skirts and white shirts for Capri pants and colorful tops. We have sunblock on our noses and sunglasses over our eyes. As she predicted, her hair is squashed. We are relatively alone on the deck in the stern of the ship.

"I'm just spit balling here, but I think I'm getting this all figured out. Remember when we were in Ketchikan and we saw Sean talking to a tall man, and later I realized that tall man was Colin? And then Phoebe told us she had seen Sean talking to Brittany? And how we learned the room where the séance was held actually belonged to the crew? It's all falling into place. I'll bet Brittany is Madam L'Oeil, and she was able to use that room because Colin is part of the crew. She brought the snow globe to the consignment store. Maybe she uses the name of Irina when she's with crewmembers."

Olivia looks doubtful. "Then why is Brittany a passenger? And she is because I see her all over the place."

"Maybe they are on a working vacation. He's working, and she's vacationing. I should probably say she's also working since they are both obviously up to something evil. I'll bet they're involved with Grant Merino in this art forgery stuff. What better way to get fake art onboard than to have a crewmember bring it? Didn't Brittany say she was now involved in the theater? She could easily have played the part of the phony medium." I clap my hands. "I remember her saying 'y'all.' At the time, it didn't mean anything, but it sure does now."

I'm feeling extremely satisfied. "Sean must have been onto the couple so they disposed of him somewhere. I refuse to believe he's dead. There has to be a way to get her to confess and tell us what they did with Sean."

"You scare me a little bit when you talk like that. How are we going to get her to confess? If we upset her, I'm pretty sure she could take us both out. She's looks awfully fit. Have you seen her muscles?"

"For heaven's sake, Olivia. I'm not afraid of her." Which isn't entirely true. "And we're not going to trap her using brawn. We're going to use our brains."

Olivia pulls strands of windblown hair off her face and says, "In that case, we should go find Dirk." She glances at me. "He has rational ideas."

Dirk! I forgot I'd agreed to meet him almost an hour ago. I missed our date because an hour ago we were washing dishes in the kitchen. I want to assure Olivia that I, too, have rational ideas, but considering the activities of a while ago, she probably wouldn't believe me.

"I agree with you. Let's go find him."

Dirk and his sister, Elizabeth, are having tea in the Sandbox Café. They each have hand-painted porcelain pots of tea and are sharing a lazy Susan with small cucumber sandwiches. It looks very civilized, and I'm aware I have glue on my fingers and glitter in my hair.

Dirk looks up at me. "Arts and crafts day?"

"Something like that." I scoot in next to him and hide my hands in my lap. "I've made some great discoveries, and I couldn't wait to share them." I glance at his sister.

"Sorry, Elizabeth. I'm just so excited, I have to tell someone."

She smiles. "No, go ahead. Dirk's been telling me some of the details, and it all sounds fascinating."

I'm trying to keep a smug smile off my face. "It's just that I've figured everything out, and now I need Dirk to help me wrap up the case."

Dirk's lower lip begins to quiver, and I realize he's trying to swallow a smile. "I can't wait to hear this. What have you got?"

So I tell them about Brittany and Colin being the bad guys and how Colin actually works on the ship and how Brittany has to be Madam L'Oeil. He doesn't interrupt me, and when I finish he says, "Can you prove any of this?"

"Well, no. That's where you come in. You're good at interrogation, but don't worry, I'll do all the dirty work until the perps are ready for questioning."

Now he laughs. "That statement terrifies me. You're not going to rough anyone up, are you?"

Actually, even I don't know why I said what I did. Tony didn't talk that way, and he was a cop. Probably too much TV. "Please don't make fun of me," I say sheepishly. "I know I'm on to something."

He pushes his plate away and puts his napkin on the table. "I think you are, too. It's interesting to think Colin might be part of the crew. Would it do any good to ask you to not approach the Bannings until I've had time to talk to someone?"

I consider this. "How much time would you need?"

"Half an hour, forty-five minutes tops if I can find the right guy. I'll meet you in the lounge across from the art gallery. In the meantime, go take a nap or something. Do we have a deal?"

I nod, but I have my fingers crossed behind my back. I'm not going to take a nap. I'm going to go find Brittany.

After searching the exercise room and places on the Sport Deck, I spot Brittany outside, walking the loop from bow to stern. I sigh and start after her, but honestly, doesn't this woman ever sit down and read a book or something? She doesn't look happy as I fall into step next to her.

"What now, Julia? I'm trying to exercise."

"Super. We can do that together."

She speeds up until we are both jogging. I know I'm not going to be able to keep this up for very long, so I talk fast.

"Where's your husband? I never see him around anymore."

"He's at an investment seminar. We're very conscious of intelligent financial planning."

Whoa! This doesn't sound like the woman who burbled about being a Dallas cheerleader. This woman sounds smart. Where was he yesterday?"

She stops walking. "I have no idea where he was. I don't keep track of all his movements. What's it to you? Why all the questions about my husband?"

"Just wondering," I say casually. "Tell me, do you enjoy séances?" Dirk would have a fit if he knew I just asked that, but he isn't here, and I'm trying hard to forget he told me to stay away from the Bannings.

"Why on earth would I be interested in séances? Are you sure you're feeling well? I'm not enjoying this conversation."

"I'm just curious. Do you believe in mediums and talking to people on the Other Side? I, personally, think it's all hokum, but a lot of people think it's possible to connect with dead loved ones. They say some mediums use crystal balls or crystal ball…ah…substitutes."

I'm getting to her. Her hands are fluttering ever so slightly, and there's a thin line of sweat on her forehead that isn't from jogging. "I think you're crazy. You need to go somewhere for a rest. I'd like to end this, Julia. I don't want to talk anymore."

I smile. "But I do. I know all about Madam L'Oeil's real identity. Tell me, how does she get all her information?"

"I have absolutely no idea what you're talking about." Brittany is visibly upset and her eyes swivel around looking for help. I'm about to go in for the kill and tell her I know everything, but someone taps me on the shoulder and a voice say, "Hi, Julia, could I speak to you for a minute?"

Dirk is frowning so severely his eyebrows almost touch, and, of course, as soon as he appears, Brittany makes her escape.

"Why did you do that? I had her. She was about to confess." I like Dirk a whole lot—in fact, a very very whole lot, but I wish he could, just sometimes, go with the flow. Spontaneity goes out the window when he's in his lawyer mode.

"Sorry, but I wanted to tell you what I found out about Colin before we tackle Brittany. I think you'll be interested."

Mollified, I un-purse my lips and say, "Tell me what you've got."

"Okay. Colin does, indeed, work on the ship. It's unusual for this shipping line to hire Americans, but Colin was able to persuade the higher ups he was a good chef. He graduated from the Culinary Institute of America. The waters got a bit murkier when I asked about his marriage. That fact doesn't seem to be in his papers. So Brittany is either his girlfriend or his wife. It doesn't much matter. I asked about her. She's a paying guest, and he would be allowed to visit her. He was only recently hired on and insisted he had to have the Alaska trips because of an ill parent in Juneau."

I am gobsmacked—as they say in England. "That's certainly not what he told us. He said he was a football coach in Texas. Why would he do that?"

"People do funny things when they're away from their normal routine. Maybe he was embarrassed about being part of the crew. Maybe he and Brittany concocted their story together to make them look more appealing. Or maybe Brittany didn't want anyone to think she was with someone from the kitchen crew. Keeping up such an elaborate deception would be hard work, but you know what they say—different strokes for different folks."

I consider this. "So maybe Brittany was never a Dallas Cowboys cheerleader."

"Maybe not." Dirk is sometimes a man of few words.

"But I still think she's L'Oeil. The snow globe the fake medium used is down in the crew quarters thrift shop. She would have had access to it through Colin."

"Very true."

My head is beginning to hurt. "This is all very confusing. Maybe Brittany and the snake oil salesman are in the forgery business together, and Colin doesn't know anything about it. Brittany is simply using her boyfriend/husband."

By now Dirk and I have walked the length of the deck and are now leaning against a rail. The sun is warm on our faces, and the blue sky, sparkling water, and mountains in the distance are mesmerizing. I close my eyes and wish I could forget all about Sean, Grant Merino, Brittany and Colin Banning, fake mediums, Isabella, and the dead Antonio Romano. This sure is turning out to be a cruise to remember.

My phone is pinging in my pocket. I pull it out and see a text from Isabella. It's brief and to the point. *Can you come?*

Baby Sophia is lying on her back in the Pack and Play. She is smiling at a mobile of colorful animals above her head. Isabella is wringing her hands. Without speaking, she gives me a piece of paper and watches me read the message.

"Don't talk about your husband, or your baby won't have a mother."

Lordy! This is terrible, but I try to keep my expression neutral. "Isabella, do you understand what this says? Capisci?"

"Si." She points to a laptop on the bed. "I Google."

The Internet is a wonderful thing. You can instantly translate hateful threats in any language. She begins to cry, so I put my arm around her and tell her not to worry, which is patently a lie, but it won't do her any good to know that.

"It will be okay," I say. "Someone is trying to scare you, but we won't let anything happen to you or Sophia." As I speak I wonder how, exactly, I intend to prevent that. I also wonder who would be despicable enough to do this to a young widow. I'm praying she and the baby will be safe until the ship docks in Seattle tomorrow.

As I make my way back to my room, my mind is spinning like a Rolodex. There is simply too much going on. My busy brain flips past forgeries, murder, and missing Sean and stops at Dirk. I honestly never thought I'd see him again, and now my heart is in a bit of a turmoil. I'd cut him out of my life for two simple reasons: 1. I didn't want to get hurt in the likely event he would find someone younger, prettier—and most importantly—geographically closer. And 2. I didn't want another man I loved to die on me. Back when I stopped taking his phone calls, I figured it was easier to live alone than risk all that. Now, I'm not so sure. We haven't had enough time on this trip to make any plans for the future, but there's no denying there is definitely chemistry between us. Yes, he annoys me when he's so analytical and so convinced he's right about everything, but I probably have little habits that annoy him, too. I can't imagine what they would be, but everyone has some faults. So should we give it another shot? If I don't make up my mind soon, tomorrow when we say goodbye in Seattle will be the last time we see each other. After this cruise, I don't think I'm planning on taking another one.

I wait for the elevator on the Promenade Deck, and when the door opens, I almost don't step in. The snake oil salesman and a passenger are standing at the rear. I do, though, and stand as close to the front as possible. He nods curtly to me and goes back to his conversation, and since I'm so close, I can't help listening. They are discussing prints by Monet, Renoir, and Dalí, and I'm surprised at what I hear. Grant Merino just said, "Yes, Renoir's work is a wonderful example of art from the Art Deco period."

Everyone who knows even a little bit about art knows Renoir was a very famous French Impressionist. How on earth could the art director of a gallery make such a mistake? Just to reassure myself that nearly everyone knows the artist, I text Olivia.

"Who is Renoir?"

Her answer comes instantly. "He sells sushi on White Street in Wake Forest."

I'm about to chastise her for her answer when she texts, "He was a French Impressionist. Why don't you know that? You're the art person."

Does this make Olivia more knowledgeable about art than Grant Merino? That's a scary thought, but it certainly looks that way.

"Julia,

Do you have any news for me about Sean? I did something I probably shouldn't have done, but I'm so worried I couldn't help myself. I went through his desk looking for a hint about his job on the ship. I found several art books in one of the drawers—mostly about Picasso, Miro, and Matisse—but nothing else. His laptop isn't here, so I assume he took it with him Did you happen to see it in his room? I know the ship docks in Seattle tomorrow. He has to come home. Please figure out what happened to him.

Courtney"

"Hi, Courtney,

I wish I had something good to tell you. I don't, but in this case I think no news is good news. I do feel we're getting close to some answers. I didn't see his laptop in his room. Did I tell you I did find his phone? It was wedged between the cushions of a chair. It won't help, though, because it's locked. Please try not to worry. We'll get this all sorted out, and he'll be home before you know it.

Julia"

Why do I say things like that? I honestly have no idea when/if we're going to find Sean. I just can't bear to hurt that nice lady.

CHAPTER TWENTY-FIVE

My dress for the Fancy Dress Ball is an ice blue, slinky silk number that resembles a nightgown but is what the salesperson assured me is elegant evening wear. I don't know what I was thinking. It looked fabulous in Dillard's dressing room mirror, and the enthusiastic lady helping me said I looked stunning. But I'm bulging—even with Spanx holding me in so tightly I can hardly breathe.

Olivia eyes me critically. "I told you to lay off all the food and lattes, but you just laughed and said food you eat on a cruise doesn't count."

She, of course, looks fabulous. She's wearing an long emerald green dress that hugs her body in all the right places. There are no bulges. Her hair is swept up and held in place by a cascade of tiny pink roses. And on her feet are gold, strappy high-heeled sandals.

I've done the best I can with my hair, and it looks pretty good. It's amazing what hairspray can do. I, too, am wearing six-inch heels, which threaten to topple me with each step. Still, I'm excited. "This is like going to prom," I say to Olivia.

"Good grief! You really are acting like a schoolgirl. This is simply a dance on a ship. There will be a lot of phony chatter from a lot of sweaty people we'll never see again."

I'm hoping that's not true, because I do want to see Dirk again, but I don't share that with Olivia. Instead, I pick up my mask and inspect it one more time. It's beautiful, and my artistic talents came in handy. Its basic color is blue, the color of my dress, and there are lavender, deep blue, and silver sequins and glitter. Plumes of blue and violet feathers flutter from each side. I hold it in front of my face, look in the mirror, and think my appearance is quite exotic.

Olivia's mask is a deep lavender with green sequins and glitter and reminds me of cat eyes. She doesn't have any plumage, but she still looks sensational. I give my face one more swipe of blush and a bit of lip gloss and pick up my gold evening bag.

"Shall we go?"

"You're twitching like a nervous girl on her first date," Olivia says. "I just hope the music is good."

The Atrium on the Promenade Deck has been transformed into a sparkling fairyland. Tall fake pine trees that weren't there this afternoon line the perimeter, and silver ribbons and balls hang from the branches. Hidden white lights twinkle in the foliage. In one part of the room is a champagne tower. Special glasses are carefully arranged in ten tiers with one glass remaining at the top. The server pours champagne into this glass, and it miraculously cascades down until all the glasses are filled. This is probably something I shouldn't try at home. At the far end of the Atrium round tables have been arranged in a semicircle around the dance floor.

Many passengers are wearing costumes, which I recognize come from the ship store. Others are dressed in elegant evening wear. I catch my breath as I spot Dirk across the room. He's standing near the buffet table talking to Elizabeth, and there are already women circling him like hungry piranhas. My feet are already killing me, but I manage to mince over to him without screaming in pain. My whole ensemble depends on the proper footwear, so I'm just going to have to suck it up.

He smiles when he sees me. "Feet hurt?"

"Absolutely not. Why do you ask?"

"I'm not going there. You look wonderful tonight."

I jiggle the mask in front of my face. "How do you know who I am?"

"I recognize the body—and you're standing next to Olivia who isn't wearing a mask."

Since we're also standing next to the buffet table, I figure it won't hurt to have a look. The servers haven't finished bringing out all the food, but so far it looks good. There's smoked salmon with lemon wedges, platters of oysters on the half shell sitting in ice to keep them cold, beef Wellington, sautéed prawns, grilled mushrooms, and other side dishes.

Dirk sees me looking and says, "Are you hungry?"

"Not really, but if we want to eat, we should probably be here when the buffet opens. These people swarm around food like ants at a picnic."

Dirk laughs. "Again, not going there. Why don't we dance?"

he band is playing "Wind Beneath My Wings." Dirk takes me in his arms, and I snuggle into his body. He smells and feels good. How could I have been so stupid? Of course, I want to be with this man. As we dance, I look at the other folks twirling around us. A vampire with what looks like real fangs is wearing a black cape and dancing with a woman dressed in a fairy costume. The poor thing keeps ducking to avoid being stabbed with the fangs.

Melissa's costume is unfortunate. She chose to dress as a German milkmaid and is wearing a green dirndl with white puffy sleeves, a rose apron, and a tinkling bell around her waist. A yellow wig with Pippi Longstocking pigtails completes her outfit. Tina is dressed as an elf.

"So many people are wearing costumes," I murmur. "I'm glad we didn't. Did I tell you how awful they smell?"

Dirk holds me tighter. "I believe you did. Stop talking now."

Olivia and Grant dance by, and she makes a face as they pass us. He's wearing a tux and looks quite presentable. I'm hoping she doesn't say anything about the doodles.

A woman wearing a full skirt, purple blouse, a shawl around her shoulder, and bangle bracelets on her wrist taps me on the shoulder.

"Having fun?"

"Excuse me." I smile tentatively. "Do I know you?" The woman has a heavily made-up face with lots of smoky eye shadow and bright red lips. Her hair is long, straight, and shiny black.

The woman laughs. "It's me. Brittany. This is such fun playing another role. Toodles."

She sashays away before I can identify her dance partner. It isn't Colin. There isn't anyone in the room tall enough to be Colin, and anyway, I know where he is. He's in the kitchen creating the lovely food.

"This is all beginning to make sense," I say to Dirk. I'm so excited I have to consciously restrain myself from clapping him on the shoulder. "Brittany is Madam L'Oeil, and I should have known it right away. I remember her telling me how much she enjoyed playing character roles. And now she appears dressed as a gypsy just to taunt me because she obviously doesn't think I'm smart enough to figure this out. Grant Merino is selling fake art. His accomplice is Brittany, and she may be the one who brings the art onboard. That makes sense because, as Colin's wife or whatever, she could have access to the crew quarters. Somehow poor, innocent Antonio stumbled upon them doing their nefarious dealings, and they killed him. And Sean was on the ship because he was tracking down art forgers. I haven't yet figured out what they've done with him." I gulp. "Maybe they've killed him, too, but I'm hoping not."

"How much champagne have you had to drink?" Dirk asks. "I'm thinking maybe we need some food."

I haven't had enough champagne to chase the thoughts out of my head, but I willingly follow him to the buffet table. Now they've added Alaskan crab legs and several appetizing salads to the scrumptious banquet. Against my better judgment, I load my plate with crab legs and fill another one with smoked shrimp and raw oysters. Crab legs are messy to eat, but I'm not leaving Alaska without devouring some. Dirk eyes my plate and shakes his head.

"Can you eat all that?"

"It's not that much. The crab legs take up a lot of room."

Once again he tries to smother a smile.

"I don't really eat that much, you know. It just looks that way because the food I like is…well…bulky."

"I see."

"I don't want to talk about it now," I say primly.

We find places at a table and sit down. I'm delighted to see Phoebe and Martin Skofield are sitting across from us. She looks lovely in a rose, floor-length sleeveless gown. And she looks much happier than the last time I saw her. As we chat for a bit, I see Brittany bounce into view. I lean across the table and say, "Have you seen Brittany?"

When Phoebe says no, I point her out. "She's dressed as a gypsy—or maybe a medium."

Phoebe stands up for a better look. "I see her, and I see where you're going with this, but I'm not sure. Why would she dress like that if she really is Madam L'Oeil? She has to know we'd recognize her."

I wipe drawn butter off my chin. "Because she's toying with us. That's why."

I see Dirk sending me all kinds of signals with his eyes, but I ignore them.

"Are you going to confront her?"

"Not right now. We're still trying to get more info."

Phoebe looks puzzled. "Who's we?"

I finally realize I should stop talking. And once again Dirk comes to my rescue. He stands up and extends his hand. "Hi, I'm Dirk Harrison. I'm an old friend of Julia's. We were just saying it's too bad the cruise is almost over. It's been so much fun."

I can see all kinds of questions crossing Phoebe's mind, but she's too polite to ask. And excuse me, but did he just say this cruise has been fun? A man is missing, a man is dead, and another is selling fake art, and there's much more scary stuff. And while the crab legs were tasty, they weren't particularly fun to eat. Even the thick napkin won't get the butter off my hands.

"I'm going to the restroom," I tell them. "Back in a minute."

The restroom outside the Atrium is crowded. I don't need to wait for a stall because I don't intend to do anything that requires sitting down. I need the privacy of my room to wrestle the Spanx down my body, so I wash my hands in the sink and prepare to leave. I'm not quite sure what happened next. There are lots of women coming and going, and I'm not paying attention to anyone. When someone thrusts a piece of paper in my hand, I at first think it's someone's used paper towel. I almost throw it out, but something makes me look at it. The words are printed in capital letters in black ink.

"WANT TO SEE YOUR FRIEND? COME TO DECK 4 AND COME BY YOURSELF. DON'T TELL ANYONE OR YOU WON'T SEE MR. MAUER ALIVE AGAIN."

I back against the restroom wall and read the note again. I can feel my heart suddenly beating fast in my throat. I absolutely do want to see my friend, but should I tell Dirk and have him come with me? I have to admit I'm slightly afraid to meet the person responsible for Sean's disappearance. On the other hand, what if the person is watching me right now, and possibly watching Dirk, too. If I call Dirk right now, and he suddenly runs to meet me, wouldn't that tip off the unknown person?

I make a deal with myself. I'll go into the ball and see if I can spot Dirk. If I can, I'll calmly walk up to him, calmly tell him about the note, and calmly ask him for help. If I can't find him, I'll go by myself—probably not very calmly.

Unfortunately, Dirk is nowhere to be seen. Am I being paranoid or are eyes following me? I see Elizabeth dancing with a nice-looking ship's officer. Olivia is talking to two men considerably younger than she, but there's no Dirk.

I turn and head to the elevator.

CHAPTER TWENTY-SIX

I step out of the elevator and cautiously look around. There's no one down here. Even the infirmary is dark. And it's very quiet. I tell myself I'll wait five more minutes, and if no one shows up, I'm going back to the ball. This could be another effort to scare the pants off me, and if that's the case, it's working.

I nearly jump out of my shoes when my phone pings. There's a message from Dirk.

Tried to call you. Why aren't you answering? Where are you? I've looked all over. Just got a message from Courtney. She gave me the code for Sean's phone. We should have a look. Please get back to me.

Sean's phone? Where did I put Sean's phone? I remember coming back to the room and being very tired and realizing his phone was locked and basically of no use. But what did I do with it? I close my eyes and try to think. Before I went to his room I'd been rearranging my clothes. My suitcase was open…and I tossed the phone into my evening bag—the evening bag I'm holding in my hand.

I text Dirk. *I have the phone. What's the code?*

The code is 3291. Julia, WHERE ARE YOU? Please tell me. I am getting worried.

I text: *No need to worry. Trust me.* I know that's going to make him laugh.

I pull Sean's phone out of my bag and with shaking fingers punch in 3291. It opens to a document that Sean must have been reading before he disappeared. I don't know what I was expecting to see. The answer to all the mayhem on the ship? The name of the person responsible for the forgeries? Never in a million years did I expect to see this. I'm looking at a warrant for a person wanted for forgery, extortion, robbery, and much more. There's even a picture. She looks younger than she does today, but there's no mistaking the identity of the person. It's our Melissa. There's her photo and her date of birth and a list of charges against her. I read about forged checks, extortion, stolen identities, and much more before my eyes begin to blur. She has apparently been a criminal for a long time because the photo is of a much younger Melissa. Her hair is blonde, and she isn't quite as plump as she is now, but it's still Melissa.

call Dirk, but his phone rings and rings and finally goes to voicemail. I know I'm screaming when I yell, "Dirk, I got into Sean's phone, and the bad guy is Melissa. Please go find her. I'm down here on…"

I don't get any further because I hear the tinkle of a little bell and feel something hard poking me in the back. I turn around to see a grinning Melissa. Her yellow wig is askew and red lipstick is smeared over her mouth, and I wonder for a second what she's been doing.

"You've been a colossal pain in the ass, Julia. Now I suppose I have to take care of you, too. Why on earth do you care so much about the man in the room next to us? I know even your friend, Olivia, doesn't understand. Why couldn't you have just enjoyed your little cruise?" She scratches her head with the barrel of the gun. "This damn thing itches."

"Did you get it at the costume store?" I'm hoping it has lice in it.

"You've been quite nosy. I've been following you all over the ship, so I've seen you talking to that little girl on Deck 5 and the woman who lectures about whales. I even know you managed to get down to the crew quarters."

In spite of the gun pointed at my stomach, the remark about the "little girl" makes me angry. "Isabella is not a 'little girl.' She's a mother, and now she's a widow. You should be ashamed of yourself. You're a horrible person."

She cackles. "As if I care what you think about me."

"What did you do to Sean? I know you hurt him. And believe me, Melissa, I'm not the only one who knows this."

"You want to see him? I think I can arrange that."

I want to ask more, but I guess Melissa isn't interested in chatting because she comes toward me wielding the butt of her gun, and the lights go out.

It is cold and very dark. I'm lying on my back on something metal. When I try to sit up, I immediately bang my head. I can't stretch my arms or my legs either. And the side of my face is throbbing. I'm too dazed for rational thought, but I do realize I'm confined in some sort of box. It takes me forever to figure out where I am. I blame it on the extreme cold, which is not only causing me to shiver but is also making my head feel worse. My stomach heaves when the realization hits me, and I force its contents back where they belong. Throwing up on my back would be bad. But I am terrified because I know I'm in one of those drawers in the morgue.

I use my fists to bang against the sides and yell, but even as I do it, I know no one can possibly hear me. No one knows where I am, so no one will come looking for me. When Olivia and Dirk are sure I'm missing, they'll search all the decks, but no one will search the morgue. Why should they? The morgue is locked, and they don't have a key. I think the cold is making part of my brain freeze because I can't figure out how Melissa got in here. And then I remember the key I tossed on the floor. She said she'd been following me. I'll bet she found it and kept it.

I wish I had a pillow. If I'm going to die, I would like to be comfortable. It's amazing what goes through your head when you think you only have minutes to live. I will probably see Tony soon, but I really don't want to. I mean, I love him and all that, but I'd rather bake cupcakes and argue with Olivia.

I will probably have to be embalmed. When it's Olivia's turn to die, she'll be all ready because she has so much Botox and fillers in her face. Every time she has a treatment, she laughs and says she's embalming early. She made me swear never to mention her cosmetic procedures, but under these circumstances she'll probably forgive me. And if she doesn't? Oh, well.

I wonder if she'll be able to run Little Bites by herself or if she'll sell it and move away. And Dirk? I really blew it there. Speaking of Dirk gives me a glimmer of hope. If he got my message, he knows about Melissa.

At least I'll look good when they find me. I'm glad I'm wearing a fancy gown instead of my usual jeans and a T-shirt. Do I still have my shoes? They were expensive, and I'd hate to lose them. I move my foot and discover the strappy heels are still on my feet. Good. The dress looks like a nightgown without the sandals. And my evening bag with Sean's phone? Is it still here? Surely Melissa took it when she …ah…interred me. But she didn't. I move my foot, and it touches the bag.

I'm cold. Really cold. I should have worn something with sleeves. I think my skin is sticking to the cold metal, which reminds me of cartoons of an idiot putting his tongue on a freezing pole. This makes me laugh.

I'm pleased at how calm I am. Must be the lack of oxygen. And I'm proud of myself. Death with dignity and all that. I cross my hands over my stomach the way people in coffins do on TV. There's no use screaming because no one can possibly hear me, so I shall approach the light calmly.

In fact, I think I see it already, and I must be going quickly because the light is growing brighter right beyond my toes. Funny—I always thought I'd walk into the Great Beyond—not enter feet first. And voices are calling. Are they the archangels arriving to escort me upward? One of them is slapping my legs. That can't be right.

"Julia! Are you still alive? Talk to us."

I'm confused. Dirk and Olivia are here. Who is going to run the business if we both go to the Other Side? And Dirk?

"You don't have to go, too," I manage to croak. "You stay here and do your lawyer thing, although I do appreciate the gesture. You can come with me, Olivia." I mean, we've gone through everything else together. Might as well stay that way.

"What on earth are you talking about?" Dirk pulls the tray out and suddenly several faces are peering down at me. "Can you stand up? Let's get that circulation going."

I can't feel my legs, but I stand up and allow many hands to rub my arms and legs. The hands belong to people I don't know. I tap one of them on the shoulder.

"Who are you?"

"We're from the infirmary," a nice woman says. "When your friends realized where you might be, they came to us for a key." She looks embarrassed. "We seem to have lost one of them, but happily, we have a spare."

Slowly warmth comes back in my body, and my brain unfreezes. I have to show Sean's phone to Dirk. When I dive into the drawer to retrieve it, Olivia yells, "Get her, Dirk! She's trying to go back."

Dirk has me around the waist and is gently pulling me away, but I have the evening bag. I hold it up and say, "Relax, people. A lady never leaves home without her purse."

CHAPTER TWENTY-SEVEN

It's 2:47 in the morning, and I'm sitting on my bed wrapped in a blanket. I'm wearing flannel pajamas, a sweatshirt, socks, and a jacket, and my insides still feel like popsicles. There is also a bandage on the side of my head, covering the gash Melissa's pistol made. I'm still astounded they were able to find me. I owe my life to Olivia. Dirk had no idea what I meant when I left the message that said I was "down here," but Olivia immediately thought of the morgue, which shows how in sync we are.

Now Dirk is on his cell phone, and Olivia is trying to feed me hot tea. I don't want tea. I want to know if anyone has found Melissa.

Dirk ends his call and says, "No luck so far. The first response team is looking for her. They've searched her room, and all her clothes are still there, but no sign of her. Or Tina."

This is ridiculous. "She can't be that hard to find," I say. "She's wearing a yellow wig and a milkmaid dress. She should be easy to spot."

"They're doing their best, Julia, but it takes time. Do you have any idea how many rooms there are on this ship?"

"We dock at 6:30. If they don't find her by then, she'll sneak off the ship and get away."

Dirk eases me back against the pillows. "How about trying to get some sleep? Olivia and I are going to go talk to Brittany and Phoebe. Maybe they know something that will help."

My head hurts and my brain feels fuzzy. He shouldn't be talking to Brittany because she's Madam L'Oeil. Isn't she? I must have said that out loud because Dirk smiles and says, "Please stop worrying. You forget I'm a lawyer. I won't give anything away."

As soon as they leave, I lock the door and get back in the bed, but my mind doesn't want to relax. Unrelated thoughts are whipping through my brain. For instance, did we pay the electric bill at Little Bites, where will Isabella stay in Seattle, who was moving stuff in Sean's room, where is my evening dress? My mind goes back to Sean's room, and suddenly I know how the person got in there. I remember a steward telling me the privacy panels separating the verandas could be unlocked. Melissa must have persuaded our steward to open the one between her room and Sean's. He was a single man traveling alone. It probably wasn't the first time the steward had heard the request. She was able to rummage through his belongings without being seen. So Melissa is responsible for his disappearance. What did she do with him? Are she and Sean together? If so, the hiding place has to be big enough for both of them.

I close my eyes and try to think. Where do you hide on a cruise ship? They will search every room, every closet, the crew quarters, all the decks and lounges. But they haven't found her, so she's hiding somewhere. Somewhere no one will guess. Suddenly my eyes fly open because I know where she is. I bound out of bed, stick my feet into my slippers, wrap the blanket more securely around my shoulders, and head for the Promenade Deck.

There are still people dancing in the Atrium. An older man dressed as a cowboy and carrying a bottle of wine walks past me with a young woman in a nurse outfit. I hear him say something about playing doctor in his cabin. Yuck!

I push the heavy door open and step outside. A chill wind is blowing, and if I weren't intent on my mission, I'd go back inside. It is definitely not a night for a pleasant stroll. I put my head down and head to my destination.

The lifeboats on the Golden Eagle remind me of the heavy plastic kennels folks use to transport dogs—except these are two stories high, hold one hundred and fifty people and don't have a metal grill and a water bowl at the entrance. There is a proper door and windows. I'm now standing below the one Antonio supposedly landed on. I've seen crewmembers access these lifeboats via a ladder at the side, but in the dark I can't see it. There also isn't any light coming from the interior, so if Melissa is in there, she's sitting in the dark.

I turn on my flashlight and play it around the lifeboat. I see the ladder but don't know how I'm going to reach it, encumbered as I am by the blanket and layers of clothes.

I ditch the blanket and try to reach the ladder. It looked easy when I watched a crewmember do it, but it takes me several tries until I'm firmly standing on the rungs. My hands are sweaty I can hardly hold onto the railing. At least I'm not cold anymore.

I gingerly make my way to the door. Fortunately, common sense returns as I prepare to open it. What do I think I'm doing? If Melissa is in there, she's responsible for a good bit of mayhem and maybe even murder, and I'm about to walk in as if I'm going to tea. This is a seriously bad idea. I need to find Dirk and tell him my suspicions. He can get someone from the first response team to check out the lifeboat. Someone with a gun.

But sometimes the best laid plans go terrible wrong. The door opens, a head wearing a yellow wig pokes out, as does the hand with the gun.

"Well, now that you're here, come on in. May I say I'm surprised to see you. How did you get out of the morgue?"

I don't say anything because I'm too scared to speak. I do, however, step into the lifeboat because I'm not going to argue with a person holding a gun. I'm immediately almost overcome with a terrible odor.

"Lordy!" I say, trying not to gag. "This smells just like the laundry room on Deck 9 the night we sailed from Ketchikan. What have you done?"

"I didn't do it." She waves the gun into the darkness. "Tina sprayed your friend there with Skunk. It's a mixture of baking powder, yeast, and some other stuff she found. It's not toxic, but it sure stops people in their tracks. We're having a little trouble getting rid of the smell." She looks me up and down. "I don't suppose you have any ketchup on you. I read that's useful in these situations."

She is absolutely crazy, but I'm not going to mention that now. I follow the direction of her pistol and see a dark heap lying motionless. "Is that Sean? Is he alive?" I try to go to him, but she hauls me back.

"Not so fast, sweetheart. He isn't going anywhere and neither are you." She pushes me forward until I'm next to the covered heap that is Sean. Now have a seat, and let's chat. Your buddy there is fine—just asleep. We give him sleeping pills. Every once in a while, he wakes up and we feed him. We're not animals, you know."

As my eyes adjust to the darkness, I notice the inside of the lifeboat is filled with benches, and there are enough to hold one hundred and fifty passengers. We're sitting on one of them. I'm shaking—either from fury or fear—but whatever it is has loosened my tongue.

"We're on to you. Dirk knows all about your illegal activities. We're well aware of your art forgeries. Did you really think those pathetic doodles would fool someone?"

"They've fooled enough people. And I think you're hurting Tina's feelings."

At the mention of her name, Tina steps out of the shadows. In the eerie light, Tina looks like a ferret. I never noticed that before.

"Be quiet. Tina's going to tie you up. She's quite good at knots. She's also good at drawing. I'll bet you never guessed she drew the doodles."

In spite of being terrified, I say, "I certainly knew right away they were drawn by someone with no artistic ability. I feel sorry for the folks who bought them."

This earned me a sharp yank on the rope around my ankles and a caustic remark from Melissa.

"Even that dolt, Grant Merino, has no idea he's selling fakes. I can't understand how he became an art director. He knows almost nothing about art. I suppose it's due to his carnival barker personality. He hasn't spotted the other forgeries either, and I think they're quite good. Tina didn't do them." She glances at her sister. "No offense, Tina. There are a few Dalís, a Max Ernst, and two Miros. It's a very lucrative business."

She swings the gun back to me. "I have to hand it to you, Julia. Nothing I did scared you off." She cackles. "Not even Madam L'Oeil. I thought for sure that would do it."

"That was me," Tina says. "I love dressing up and pretending to be someone else. We found all the info about your husband's unfortunate murder on the Internet."

Tina has tied my hands behind my back. The rope around my wrists is too tight and is making my hands tingle. I try to wiggle my finger. "I understand trying to scare me, but why do that to Phoebe? She was terribly upset."

"Bah!" Melissa almost spits. "That woman drinks too much. She didn't even remember sitting at the bar and telling me her sob story. I thought it made the whole thing seem more realistic to have two spirits appear. Besides, Phoebe needed to be taught a lesson. Too much alcohol leads to loose lips."

"How were you able to use the room for the séance? And how did you happen to have brochures about Madam L'Oeil?" I lower my voice to a whisper. "How could you kill Antonio? He was a new father."

"We have a supply of pamphlets. Let's just say the other night wasn't our first rodeo. And we obviously have connections to the crew. I'm known as Irina, Grant's…ah…girlfriend." She stops talking, and I wonder if I've asked too many questions. Finally, she says, "The man's death was unfortunate. We didn't mean to kill anyone." She nudges Sean with her toe. "We didn't kill this one because killing a Fed is really bad."

You think? This woman is seriously deranged.

"Tina and I were down in the crew quarters putting Tina's doodles into frames, and Antonio saw us. I don't know how, but he instantly understood what we were doing and threatened to report us. He tried to run and got as far as the crew swimming pool when I hit him on the back of the head with a hammer. He fell into the water, and I guess maybe he drowned a little bit. Tina ran out on deck and yelled man overboard. That was to get people away from the pool. I fished him out, we put him in a laundry basket, went to dinner, and the ship finally stopped. You remember that dinner, don't you Julia? They couldn't find the crewmember who had yelled 'man overboard,' and the deck cameras didn't show a problem, so the ship continued. All this talking is making me thirsty. I could use a vodka soda."

"If you untie me, I'll get you one," I tell her, but she's so lost in her thoughts, she doesn't hear me.

"We knew there might be a Fed onboard. When I saw him asking Brittany questions about us, I knew I had to do something. It was, let's say, fortuitous that we had the room next to his. As soon as we sailed from Ketchikan, I knocked on his door and told him I had information about art forgeries and could he come with me immediately. Of course, he could. We went down to Deck 9 where Tina was hiding with a small canister of that awful stuff. I believe it's called Skunk. She sprayed Sean, he fell down and hit his shoulder on a metal hook. It bled, so we cut the bloody piece of cloth off his shirt. Tina didn't know what to do with it so she stuffed it in the soap dispenser. That was dumb."

"If you say so." The whole thing is dumb. I can't believe these lunatics almost got away with this. I say almost because the whole time Melissa has been lecturing, I've retrieved my cell phone from my back pocket and have been tapping it repeatedly. Dirk was the last person to call me, and I'm hoping his number is still up. I'm trying to forget there probably isn't any cell phone service in a lifeboat.

"So anyway," she says, "we were quite busy that night. We put the unconscious Fed in a laundry basket—actually the same one we later used for Antonio—waited until the middle of the night and then wheeled him up here. There's a bit of a gap in the security cameras by the lifeboats, probably because there's no room to jump overboard. I won't say it was easy wrestling him in here, but we did it."

"And Antonio? Why did you put him on top of the lifeboat?"

"That whole thing went wrong. We didn't know what to do with his body, so we decided to throw him overboard where the cameras wouldn't see us. We hoisted him to the top of the lifeboat, but his clothes snagged of some of the metal. We had to give up and leave him there. When the body was discovered, everyone thought he had jumped."

She stands up and looks at her watch. "It's 5:26 a.m. now. The ship docks at 6:30. Time to get moving. There's been a change of plans. Untie her, Tina. I need her to stand up. Don't get all worried, Julia. All I want is your pajama bottoms."

"Excuse me?"

"I'm getting off this ship as soon as we reach Seattle, and you can't expect me to wear this ridiculous costume. I'll be needing your sweatshirt, too."

As soon as I'm on my feet, she hands the gun to Tina and says, "Okay, get them off. I don't have all the time in the world. What's the matter with you? We're all girls here, and I've seen underwear before. You are wearing some, aren't you?"

I am, but I sincerely don't want to give her my clothes. She solves the problem by pushing me down on the bench and yanking the pajamas off my legs. She pulls the dirndl over her head and tosses it and the wig onto the floor. I'm glad it's dark because I really don't want to view Melissa in her skivvies.

"Now the sweatshirt?"

I have no choice. I give it to her.

"Before we go could I maybe shoot her in the feet or something?" Tina is holding the gun in both hands and pointing it at me. "She's been very annoying."

Melissa hesitates, and I know she's considering the idea.

"If I shoot her, she can't run after us."

"The idea has some merit," Melissa says, "but we don't have time for that. We're leaving now. I'm assuming you won't be running after us because you'll want to check out your friend here, plus you have no clothes." She pauses. "But on second thought, shooting you seems like a good idea. It will permanently stop you. It's been fun, Julia. Ta ta."

She aims the gun at my head, I hear a click and close my eyes. Suddenly there's a groan and a thud, and when I dare open my eyes, Melissa is on the floor, Dirk is on top of her, and he's holding Tina by one of her skinny arms.

"A little help here, Julia. If you could pick up the gun and point it at Tina, I'll take care of Melissa. And watch out. The scrawny one has sharp fingernails."

CHAPTER TWENTY-EIGHT

It is dawn and cold on the deck. Olivia and I have blankets wrapped around us as we watch the skyline of Seattle grow closer. I'm trying to drink hot coffee, but my hands are still shaking so badly, I can't get the cup to my mouth.

Dirk and Sean are standing at the rail chatting in low voices. Sean looks pale, but he's upright and talking, and that's a good sign. He woke up shortly after I found him thanks to an injection from the infirmary nurse.

"Where's Melissa?" I need to know this because I don't want her trying to kill me again. Twice is enough.

"She and Tina are in the ship's brig," Dirk says. "They'll be handed over to the police as soon as we dock."

"I have so many questions."

Dirk puts his arm around me and pulls me close. The warmth of his body feels wonderful. "I know you do, but now isn't the time to ask them. Don't you want to go to your room and take a hot shower? Or put on some clothes?" He grins. "I noticed you're missing your pants."

My clothes! I suddenly remember we were supposed to have our luggage outside the door so it could be picked up for departure. Dirk reads my mind. "Don't worry. Olivia has packed all your things and has left something for you to wear today. The captain is going to allow you to stay in your cabin as long as you like. He seems to be very grateful you uncovered the forgery ring."

A hot shower sounds like a fine idea. Olivia comes with me as I totter down the hall to our room. The door to Melissa's stateroom is wide open, and a steward is inside cleaning it for the next guests. Likewise the door to Sean's cabin. Has it only been seven days since we boarded the Golden Eagle for a splendid cruise? It seems like a lifetime. I peek into Sean's room. All his belongings are gone and everything is neat and tidy. I feel my lower lip begin to quiver, and my legs have a strange, rubbery sensation. I think I'm sagging. Olivia notices and hurries me along. "Come on, my friend. We have to resuscitate you. A shower should help."

I follow her, but I say, "I have to do one more thing. I have to see Melissa taken into custody. Otherwise I'm afraid I'm going to see her around every corner."

"Okay, but for that you're going to need some clothes."

The dock is crowded with passengers disembarking, but Sean has somehow managed to get us through the throng just as Melissa and Tina are being loaded—in handcuffs—into a police van. Melissa sees me, smiles, and tries to wave. I hear her say, "Ta ta, Julia. It was fun," before the door to the van closes and it moves away. She is nuts, and I'm pretty sure a doctor at some psychiatric facility will agree with me. I feel better now. I square my shoulders and say, "I'm hungry. Let's go eat."

Olivia and I are spending the night in Seattle because there are no flights that will get us to North Carolina today. Sean is having the same problem trying to reach his home in Pennsylvania. Even though Sacramento is only a few hours down the road, Dirk decides to stay, too. Elizabeth is anxious to get back to her practice and bids us goodbye at the hotel. We have a lovely day wandering around Pike's Place and later go to a splendid restaurant for dinner. As we settle into our seats and order some wine, I finally relax. It's over. But I need to know some stuff.

"So Sean, I know you can't tell us much, but were you on to Melissa before you boarded?"

He sips his beer and leans back. "Melissa was on our radar for a long time. She worked for a big-time forgery ring and didn't operate only on the Golden Eagle. She spent most of her time cruising on ships while distributing fake art. I was on this trip to finally stop her. Remember that day at Potlatch Park when you were in the clan house? The two people you heard whispering were Melissa and one of her forger contacts."

"And the Bannings? I was so sure bouncy Brittany was Madam L'Oeil. Was she really a Dallas Cowboys cheerleader?"

"I can answer that," Dirk says. "Brittany was a complete phony. As I told you before, some folks like to pretend to be entirely other people when they travel. Brittany was one of those. She is married to Colin—probably not happily since she flirted with lots of the men onboard—but she's harmless. I think she was just trying to put some spice into her life. She works in Accounts Receivable at an insurance company."

That makes me laugh—and somehow very happy.

"And I keep forgetting to tell you, Melissa and Tina aren't teachers at all," Olivia says.

Dirk adds, "They also aren't sisters, and they don't live on a farm outside of Akron. They don't even live together. They only meet up for their illegal scams."

"But Sean," I say, "when we were in Ketchikan, I saw Colin talking to you, and he seemed very angry. What was that about?"

"He thought I had something going with Brittany, mostly because he's seen her talking to me, and I was trying to assure him I wasn't interested. I'm a happily married man. And speaking of that…" He pulls out his phone, dials a number, and hands it to me. "Someone wants to talk to you. Both of us are thankful beyond words."

Courtney is crying, so it's hard to understand her, but I get the gist of what she's trying to say. "I think I'm as happy as you are that everything turned out fine. I can admit to you now, I was scared for a while." And I was, too. There were times I thought Sean was a goner. I assure her he looks fine and appears to be healthy. "I know he'll be happy to see you." When she says she'll send the print I ordered, I have to tell her the truth. "Courtney, I have to be honest with you. At the moment, I can't really afford the print. The cruise was expensive and…" She cuts me off.

"It's already on its way. No charge," she says. "Every time you look at it, you'll think of this cruise, so I don't know whether that's good or bad, but I want you to have it."

I thank her, give the phone back to Sean and then dig into some fabulous raw oysters. By the time we walk to our hotel, my stomach is full of delicious food, my mind is pleasantly mellow due to quite a bit of wine, and my heart is content. And what happens next at the hotel is info only Dirk and I know.

The next morning at the airport he pulls me aside and says, "I'll see you next month. In spite of everything, it's been wonderful. I thought I'd never see you again." He pulls me into a hug. "You know this is meant to be, don't you?"

It's hard to answer because my face is buried against his chest, but I manage to get out, "If you say so."

CHAPTER TWENTY-NINE

I'm in the kitchen of Little Bites creating a scrumptious lemon chiffon cake. And I'm happy. As I sift cake flour and the other dry ingredients, I remember the spotless, stainless steel pots and pans on the ship and wonder where the Golden Eagle is now. I heard Grant Merino had been relieved of his job, which is good since he had no knowledge of art. There was a big article in the Seattle paper about the FBI cracking an art forgery scheme on cruise liners. Much as I like Sean, the FBI had little to do with solving the case, but as my young niece says, "Whatevs."

Dirk has promised to keep me informed about Melissa and Tina. They're in jail in Seattle, and now that I'm in North Carolina, I feel safe. There's an entire country between us.

Dirk is coming to visit next month. This time we're taking things slow and really getting to know each other. It will be great if we end up together, but one day at a time.

Olivia swings through the kitchen door holding the mail. "Look at this offer," she says, showing me a colorful brochure with photo of camels and sand dunes. "Ten days in Morocco. We sleep in tents in the desert. Doesn't that sound exciting?"

She's got to be kidding.

THE END

ABOUT THE AUTHOR

Linda S. Clayton has been writing ever since she could hold a pencil. She wrote a poem for *Jack and Jill*, class songs, a college class play—The History of Hair, a book about her sister's many glorious hair colors and styles, and many other mostly forgettable things.

During the thirty years she and her husband lived overseas, Linda had a successful career as a portrait painter, but she never stopped writing. She wrote a humor column for an English publication in Bonn, Germany, and wrote countless attempts at novels that were shoved in the back of a drawer. Her adventures and misadventures in foreign countries are providing a steady supply of material for her new Julia Greene Travel Mysteries.

A Killer of a Cruise is the second in this series. The first is *An Ice Way to Die*.